The Beacon Star

Randy R Pischel

DEDICATION

This book is dedicated to Crystal, Jackson, Nicholas, Emma, Nehemiah, Evan, Mikela, Erica, Aaralyn, and Kaiden.

The Beacon Star

I. A Damsel in Distress

Jamison came in through the front door reluctantly. A stranger in a strange land, a fish out of water. This was such a large city, his village would fit on a single block and he'd never seen so many, well, people.

It took a few hours of asking around to find the right place. The way the old man spoke this was the only inn in the village, but there were dozens, maybe hundreds. Having to ask wasn't helping as some people just looked at him funny and others treated him like he was a simpleton. City folk just had a different attitude. But he found it and the warm fire and inviting tables made him feel a little bit better.

There was a small man sitting in a corner, picking at a plate of bread and meat. A man? Jamison wasn't sure. Otherwise the place was empty. There was a counter with a bell so he stepped up and lightly gave it a ring.

After several moments he rang it again, a little bit louder. There were some noises in back then a large, middle aged man appeared.

"Tote Putnam, at your service. What can I do for you?"

Jamison looked around a little bit, feeling nervous. "I was told to find the Beacon Star, here in Crescent. This is the Beacon Star, is it not?"

"It is. We have room and board for a weary traveler."

"Merimac sent me. He's a holy man." Putnam just continued looking at him. "Lives in the mountains east of here. He's the one who said to come here, I thought you might know him."

Putnam shook his head. "Doesn't ring a bell. But it's nice to know my reputation has traveled that far."

Feeling even more nervous now, he pressed on. "Well, he gave me this bag to give to you, told me not to look in it." He pulled a small pouch out of his backpack and set it on the counter. "He said you'd help me. He said you'd help me find a door."

Putnam picked up the bag which was much heavier than it looked. He undid the knots and looked inside then pulled a large box out from under the counter and put the bag inside. Then, much to Jamison's surprise, his eyes rolled up and gripped the sides of the box and began to mumble. His hands grew red from gripping the box so tight and the muscles in his neck stood out. Then, he put the box down and removed the bag and looked back inside.

Pushing the box aside he pulled out a black felt plate, with a high lip, and poured the bag out onto it. About 30 gold coins spilled out, each about the size of a pinky nail.

"That's a good haul," said Putnam. "And real, too. Why, each coin is about good for a week's room and board, but if you add extras I'd say you have about twenty five weeks worth here."

This brought a change in Jamison. His eyebrows curled, his jaw dropped, and it looked like someone just told him he was about to be executed.

"Twenty five weeks? No, oh no, no, no. I have to get out of here. My Cynthia was kidnapped, she's in a fortress. I need what's behind that door to rescue her. I need to…"

Putnam held his hands up to stop the boy. "Just calm down, there. No one says you're going to be here for twenty five weeks. Tell me about this door."

Taking a few deep breaths he regained his thoughts. "Merimac just told me I'd know it when I saw it. He gave me a key. Said it was on the side of a hill."

Putnam nodded. "All the doors are on the side of a hill. Haven't you ever heard of Sugar Hill?"

"No, I haven't. I'm just trying to rescue my fiance."

"Son, Sugar Hill has more magic than anywhere in all the realms. Dragons can't scratch it. It's guaranteed safe from anything. People store stuff there, people from all over the worlds. There are doors there, alright. Tens of thousands of them. I won't even try to describe it but I'll take you there in the morning."

As Jamison just stood there with his mouth opened Putnam continued. "Be here in the lobby at 7:30, have some breakfast. The wagon leaves at 8:00 or sooner if you and Mr. Beady are ready." He nodded towards the man in the corner. "We'll take you there, help with what we can and bring you back when you're ready. It's all included in your room and board. I'll put your bag in the safe, and when you leave I'll give back to you what you didn't use."

"Okay, okay, I guess."

"Now, I know you're worried about your Cynthia but just sit back, we'll get you some supper, a room, and you'll feel better in the morning."

What could he do? Jamison dropped his pack at one of the tables and sat down while Putnam disappeared into the back. He glanced at Mr. Beady, who was looking at him.

"So, where ya from?" he said in a high pitched but gravely voice.

"Oh, Farwell, it's past the mountains."

Mr. Beady went back to picking at his bread and looking out of the window where the sky was deep orange with the sunset. "Never heard of it."

*****

Too excited to eat Jamison found himself outside watching Horace, Putnam's assistant, hook up a small pony to a large wagon. Other than five rows of benches it looked like a normal wagon and it was once again nothing like Jamison had seen before.

Mr. Beady came out with Putnam but they still had to wait a few more moments as some sacks and a keg was loaded into the back of the wagon. Finally, after what seemed an eternity but still ahead of schedule, they set off.

After a few turns the roads got a little wider and the number of wagons on them got a little thicker. Jamison sat wide eyed as he had never seen so many dwarves and elves in one place, and none of them fighting. He saw women with wings and he didn't even know what they were and was afraid to ask. He even saw some gnomes and some fairies flitted by, unhindered by the wagons in the road.

Putnam glanced over his shoulder and caught Jamison staring at some of the dwarves.

"Crescent is a neutral city. No fighting is tolerated here and there are spells to prevent it. People learn quickly to just stick to their business. It's all residual of the hill."

"Why don't the wagons use the rest of the street?"

"That's for wagons coming from the other direction, we need rules to keep things moving otherwise it gets all locked up and nothing moves. Up ahead is the pedestrian lane, it's the main lane up to the gates. When we turn up there you'll see the hill. Crescent is thickest here and hugs the hill about three quarters the way around. The back is open to wilderness, not all Openers want to come in through the city."

"Openers?"

"Owners of the doors. Or people like you who are here to open one. There is a pure type of magic in the hill, it absolutely protects all the doors. Kings keep their treasures here, wizards keep their secrets, right down to brownies who sometimes keep a single acorn behind theirs. An invasion of dragons can't open a door if it wasn't meant to be. Some have been here for centuries, and they added a few just last year. It's all tricky business."

The wagon turned a corner following the other wagons and this lane was open all the way to the hill. Jamison wasn't sure what he was looking at. The part he could see through the buildings looked like a giant quilt. As they got closer his first impression appeared to be the most correct.

The hill was long and low and dotted with trees and had an old wooden water tower on the top. But there any resemblance to a normal hill ended. There were rows and rows of colorful doors that set the main pattern. In between were smaller rows, then more chaotic smaller doors of every shape from round to jagged like a lightning bolt. Jamison tried to take them all in, but there were thousands visible, and he could only imagine the pattern continued all the way around.

They passed the last building and the lane they were on opened up into a wide field covered with tall poles. Colorful flags flew from most poles and small rows of stones on the ground marked out large rectangles. It was into one of these rectangles that Horace led the little pony. At the top of a pole he could just make out the tower and star from the same Beacon Star sign from the front of the inn.

Putnam looked around at all the empty spaces. "Light day. Now, the wagon will be here most of the day. Mr. Beady knows about where he's going so we may leave for a few to take him back, otherwise you can always find the wagon here. We have bread and some pork, and a keg of beer and you are welcome to it, it's yours. Take some with you. The town clock is over there, at four bells start making your way back, we'd like to leave by five bells."

He was interrupted by a wagon passing in front of them. It was a large hay wagon and the driver asked if Putnam would be there all day, and then dropped off a few forkfuls of hay for the pony.

"Don't worry about walking on doors, you can't harm them and in places you absolutely have to. If a Guild member approaches you, don't fall for what they say, they charge for many things we can already do for you. They have their place, but check with me first." He trailed off as something caught his eye. All turned to look.

Jamison couldn't believe his eyes. "Is that an ogre?"

They watched as the ogre, who was so tall that men barely passed his waist, walked up to the gate. The gate's roof was split and lifted, like a drawbridge, as the ogre passed through. They were set up to even accommodate giants.

"Yep," said Putnam, "That is an ogre. He can't hurt anyone on the hill, of course, but I'd stay well away from him if you can. No telling what he's up to."

Mr. Beady smiled and nodded. "I'll be off, if you don't mind."

"Would you like Horace to go with you?"

"Sure, if he doesn't mind." With that Horace and Mr. Beady head out.

After they were gone Putnam spoke quietly to Jamison. "Look, I have no idea what sort of wizard you met in the woods but you could spend a long time here looking for something that 'you'll know when you see it' so set up a pattern and try not to backtrack. I'll go with you to get you started but I have some errands to run later so I can't stay all day. Do you have your key?"

Jamison nodded. "Of course." He pulled it out and apart from being slightly larger than normal it looked like a standard skeleton key with a shaped paddle at one end and a ring at the other for twisting.

"That's not a lot to go on. Let's pack a lunch for you and I'll show you a few things."

From the main gate a wall stretched around the hill with several smaller gates spaced out at irregular intervals. In some places the wall was collapsed and in others it gave way to fencing of wood or wire. It seemed more to mark the edge than to keep people out.

As they passed the wall Jamison saw the extent of how much the hill was covered in doors. Some were as large as regular doors, most were the size of cupboard doors, but in between they got smaller and smaller until some looked like they were barely big enough for a mouse.

"It still amazes me. Some are deep and have rooms, some are mere boxes, some are quite shallow. I never know what to expect behind a door. What, exactly, are you hoping to find, if you don't mind my asking?"

Jamison almost missed the question, he was hoping some door would magically jump out at him as the one he needed. He was looking at all the styles from plain wood to fancy carvings to geometric patterns of every color and every size.

"Oh, well, a map of the fortress. Mr. Merimac said he was inside before and mapped several passages that are no longer used. And a sword that is enchanted, it makes everyone in range not want to fight. We mapped out where my Cynthia may be and he said I should be able to get in and out before the alarm is raised. But the map shows other things, like the cliffs outside the fortress where we can get out and not be chased."

Putnam was just nodding, what a long shot. "Well, I wish you good luck with all that. There's a keyhole."

He pointed down to the nearest door but Jamison shook his head. Nothing jumped out at him.

"Don't be afraid to try keyholes, no one will mind."

"Isn't there a list, or map, or key that tells who owns what door? Everything else here is so organized."

"I'm afraid not. Many predate the city. Many change hands. New ones appear. Some have even disappeared. Some are known but that's only a fraction."

Putnam looked around for the ogre but he wasn't in sight.

"Well, any questions? I'll stay with you a bit. You know, just because there's a key doesn't mean there's a key hole. Maybe keep that in mind as well."

Jamison's heart was dropping. Every moment was a moment he couldn't be on his way to the fortress. Why wasn't he given more to go on? Why wasn't he told there were so many doors? How sure would he be when he saw it? He felt as if a clock was ticking in his chest and hope was fading with every tick.

*****

The next morning Jamison had skipped breakfast again and sat on the wagon waiting for Putnam and Horace to come out. He was exhausted and sore and his legs barely lifted him. Putnam stayed well past sunset even though it meant breaking his rule of coming back on time. This poor kid was desperate. Mr. Beady was sleeping in with whatever was in the bags he brought back the night before and two new guests had arrived and were eating breakfast slower than anyone Jamison had ever seen before.

At least that's how it seemed. Luckily they were not going to the hill today and Putnam and Horace came out, loaded the wagon, and they were off.

The trip to the hill was uneventful except Jamison saw his first centaurs, and wishing his fiance was there to see them only made him want to find the door even more.

The wagon rolled up to its parking spot and Putnam had to almost restrain him to keep him from running off.

"You will work better and keep a clearer head if you take food with you. You won't be doing your fiance any good if you pass out before noon." Reluctantly Jamison agreed.

While they were packing a bag a small slender man with pointed ears came up to the wagon. At first Jamison thought he was an elf, but there was something un-elvish about him that he couldn't put his finger on.

"Morning, Mr. Putnam."

"Mr. Tinker." Putnam nodded back.

"You staying late and bringing the same guest back caught the attention of the Guild. Surely there's something we can help with."

Jamison looked at Putnam hopefully. Putnam had mentioned the Guild the day before but at this point he was willing to try anything.

Putnam never trusted the Guild, they were money grubbing opportunists and the fact that a member was here simply meant no one very rich needed their help today, but he knew this kid could look for weeks and not find his door.

With a sigh he said, "Show him the key, boy. It's from a Merimac."

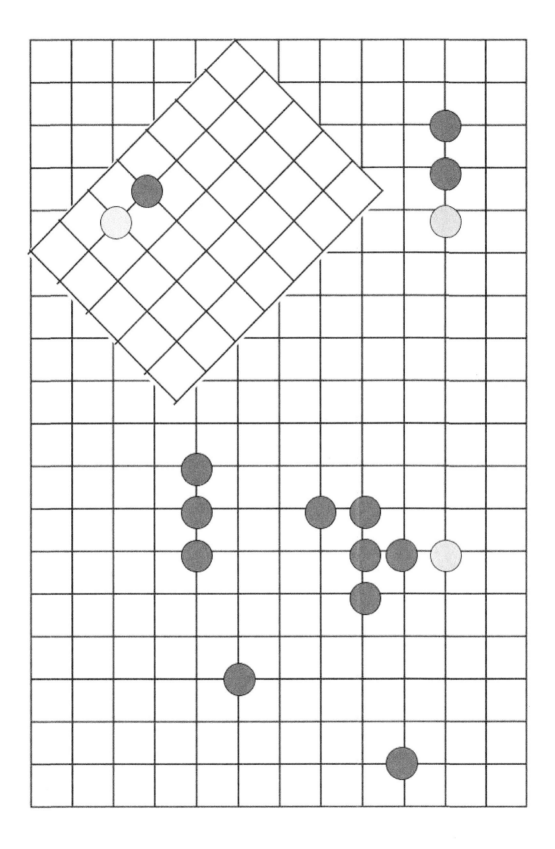

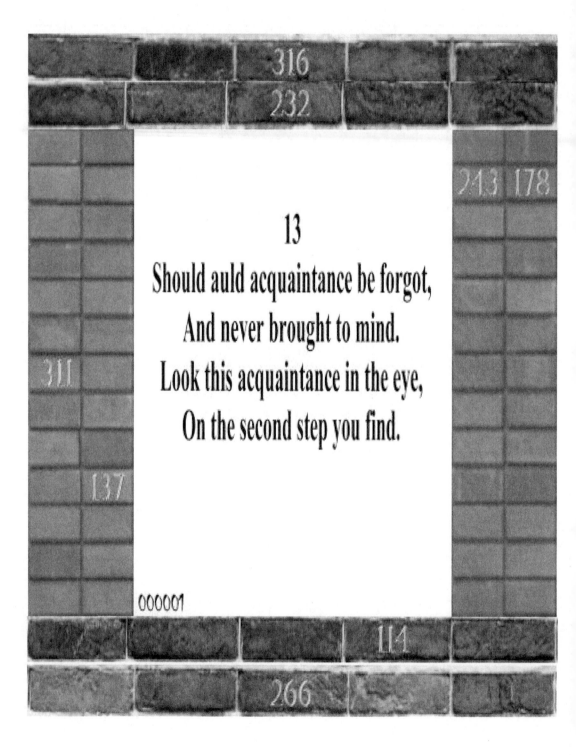

13

Should auld acquaintance be forgot,

And never brought to mind.

Look this acquaintance in the eye,

On the second step you find.

Mr. Tinker looked at the key and thought a bit. "Merimac doesn't ring a bell, but I can check the registry. What else do you know?"

"Only that I'd know it when I saw it."

Mr. Tinker gave the key back. "I can't help you with that one."

Without missing a beat, Putnam pulled a gold coin out of his pocket. "Alright, tell us what you know." Mr. Tinker took the coin and looked at it suspiciously. "It's real. From my own purse."

"Alright, I will tell you this. If this Merimac was any kind of a wizard then the spell can only be fulfilled when you look at the door and nothing else. I mean, look up at the hill, you can see thousands, why isn't yours jumping out at you? That's because you are not looking right at it and nothing else, you are seeing many at a time. You have to walk, and look down, and look at each door, one by one. If you are just glancing around the spell won't take, you have to go slow."

Jamison slowly nodded. That did make sense, but that would mean retracing some of what he did yesterday, just to be sure. His heart sank a little more but he understood a little more.

"Thank you, Mr. Tinker." It was all he could muster. He pulled the bag with food off the cart and walked towards the nearest gate.

When he was out of earshot Mr. Tinker turned back towards Putnam, then he stared at Horace and squinted his eyes. Horace got the message and wandered off.

"You know," Mr. Tinker said in a low voice, "the Guild can cover this. It's not the first time a door on sight spell has been cast."

All Putnam could say was, "I'm listening."

"This is between you and me, if this gets out we'll shun you and give your inn the mark of a snitch."

"You know I'll keep my word. On my honor as an innkeeper of the hill." It also meant Putnam would know a Guild secret, which put him another notch over other innkeepers. Mr. Tinker knew this as well and he knew there would be another innkeeper who would send business to the Guild the next time this situation arose.

Mr. Tinker indeed knew Putnam would keep his word but the warning had to be said, by a Guild member. He glanced around and carried on. "Okay, look, over the centuries we've worked out a path that can be walked so you could look at every door in the space of three days. Less if you can go around the clock. But this path is top secret."

"And how much will it take to learn this path?"

"Oh, no. He'll be led. And not by me, I'm not high enough in the Guild."

This meant the price may be too high. "Well, how much, then?"

"Take your boy home, get him some rest and food. Have him go to the water tower at midnight. There will be a guild member there who'll ask for thirty pieces of gold."

"Thirty…"

Mr. Tinker held up his hand. "Have him offer twenty, which he'll accept. The other ten will go to me, as a finder's fee."

Putnam wasn't happy. "That's still thirty pieces of gold. Do you think he's rich or something? He's trying to save a damsel in distress and the clock is ticking."

They stood for a few moments, each one just trying to wait out the other.

"Ten pieces if he finds his door, if he doesn't, no finder's fee."

"Deal."

"HORACE!" Putnam's yell nearly made Mr. Tinker fall over, which was half of what Putnam was going for.

"Good day to you." Mr. Tinker tipped his hat and left.

*****

Jamison climbed to the top of the hill with his lantern and a bag of food. Other lanterns could be seen dimly lighting the way for other door seekers in the distance.

A hooded figure stood in the dark under the water tower and Jamison had to swallow his terror at the sight of him. "Are you here to show me the way?'

It took a moment for the figure to answer, a moment in which Jamison thought he had the wrong man and was about to be skewered, forgetting that everyone was always safe on the hill.

"Thirty pieces of gold." The figures voice wasn't menacing at all, in fact it was almost childlike and put Jamison at ease a little bit. This was not the sinister voice of anything evil. He remembered his instructions and said, "Twenty."

"Twenty it is. Your canteen."

In the dim light he held out his hand and it took a moment for Jamison to realize the hooded figure wanted his canteen. He swung it off his neck and handed it to him, he wasn't about to refuse any favors to the man who may help him find his door. To his surprise the man took off the cap and poured it on the ground. "What are you…"

The hooded figure quickly held up a finger silencing him. He turned to the leg of the water tower and turned a valve on a small pipe the led up to the darkness above and quickly refilled the canteen, then handed it back.

"This entire hill is magic." The hooded figure said. "This tower was one of the first things here, built before the city of Crescent. The water retains a little magic and will sustain you beyond any food you could eat. Take a drink and concentrate, if you will know the door when you see it, then see it you shall. But first, payment."

Jamison took the little bag off his belt. He argued with Putnam but in the end accepted back 20 of the gold pieces he had originally gave for his room and board. He handed it to the figure who handed his canteen back in return. He took a swig and was amazed at how cold it was.

And refreshing.

And delicious.

"I understand you have a damsel in distress." The hooded figure said.

"Yes. We should get started."

"Before you leave you should fill all your canteens up from this tower. No one will say anything. It will help you, I think, in the long run."

"I will, I already feel it."

The hooded figure tilted his head. "Then shall we? Follow me, but watch the ground, look at each door on it's own. Look when I point at something specific. And keep the lantern bright as you can until dawn. And one last thing."

"Yes?"

"Do you have ham? I smell ham and I'd really like some."

*****

Putnam looked up from his books and watched a wagon go by out in the street. He looked back down and did a final bit of adding and frowned. "I don't like dry spells. Any word from that woman from West Creek? She's two days past her reservation."

"No word at all." Horace was keeping busy topping off the oil lamps and cleaning dust while he was at it.

"How do you feel about selling a pony? We only ever need one at a time."

"Well, we don't need three, that's for sure. We should sell some stock as well, before it goes bad. We haint been cooking much lately. Potatoes are starting to sprout."

Putnam grunted. "Well, we should just eat more. Make a big pot of stew tomorrow. I still have those rubies from the dwarves. We could almost retire for year on those."

"Just buy a bigger sign for the road, people like inns with big signs."

Just then Horace felt a strange calm come over him. He put down the oil and his rag and sat down on the bench and leaned into the corner. It was so comfortable. Just relaxing and sitting and watching the room

Putnam also relaxed, he closed his books and sat back in his padded chair and thought how nice and quiet everything was. There was a satisfaction with meeting expenses and knowing you are secure through slow times. He put his feet up and thought about how comfy he was and how he could just sit here forever.

Neither of them even jumped when the door burst open and Jamison came running in.

"I found it! I found it! I was just walking behind the Guild guy, and there it was. My key fit and we opened it and I found the map and the sword and there were boxes and stuff in there, but I left it alone because I promised I would. But I'm ready to set off!"

"That's nice." Was all Putnam could manage. It was good to have a happy customer.

"Oh." Jamison almost laughed. He put the sword on the table and as soon as he let go the room seemed to shimmer a little and Horace and Putnam both jumped to their feet.

"What in blazes just happened?"

"Oh, the sword, it really works, it calms everyone down and makes it so no one will want to fight. It even affected the Guild member who was leading me. And the guy who gave me a ride here."

Putnam came around his counter and looked closely at the sword being careful not to touch it. "Well, my hopes that you'll succeed just increased tenfold. I'm very happy for you, lad."

Jamison wasted no time. "I've got to get my things, I've got to head out." And with that he ran down the hall where the guest rooms were.

"Boss," said Horace, who had also come over to look at the sword, "It's a long way back to the mountains, and you were just saying we don't need three ponies."

Putnam nodded. "Yeah, go saddle one up."

Horace smiled and headed out the side door.

When Jamison returned he was all packed up just as he was when he arrived. "Sir, Merimac wanted me to give this bag when I left. There is a note inside."

The bag contained thirty more pieces of gold and this time Putnam didn't check them at all. He pulled out the note and unfolded it but couldn't read the letters. "This is written in elder tongue, I'll need to have it translated. But no worries, I thank you very kindly and I have something for you as well. Horace will have it out front shortly."

Without warning Jamison threw his arms around Putnam. "Thank you so much, thanks for setting me up with that Guild guy, thanks for showing me everything."

Putnam smiled. "It's alright. Go and save your lady. Come back if you have a chance, you'll always have a place to stay here."

Jamison picked up the sword and tucked it into his belt as quickly as he could. In that short time Putnam already wanted to sit on a bench and stare out the window but it passed quickly. The kid nearly knocked down Tinker on his way out, apologized, then saw Horace with the pony and went straight for another hug.

Inside Putnam looked at Tinker and smiled. "That was quick. But I'm a man of my word."

He shook ten coins out of the bag and dropped them in Tinker's already outstretched hand.

"Pleasure doing business with you. Once he left the hill that kid and his sword had half the town asleep. I had trouble following him, kept finding the most comfortable spots to sit. It wasn't destructive magic so the protection spells let it slide. Very unusual."

They watched as Horace helped arrange bags on the back of the pony.

"Say, Tinker, can you read elder tongue?"

"All Guild members can."

He handed the note to Tinker who crinkled his eyes at it. "It just says 'This is for the pony.' It's written with beetle's ink, very rare."

"Whoever that monk is who is helping this kid must be very powerful." Putnam smiled. "And he recommended my inn."

"And what do you think of the Guild now? That kid could have been up there for years."

"Well, you guys aren't so bad, I guess. Still, ten gold coins for a finder's fee..."

"And a copper for the translation."

"Get out."

Tinker didn't argue and went through the front door where Horace was still waving goodbye to Jamison, now well down the street.

"Oh, and Tinker." Putnam yelled, still inside, causing Tinker to look back over his shoulder.

"Thanks."

Horace came in shaking his head. "You thanking a Guild member. What is this world coming to?"

Putnam smiled. "Life is good, Horace, life is good."

II. A Piece of Cake

"Horace, did you make lunch?" Putnam noticed the day was getting long and he hadn't eaten yet.

"Yes, I just delivered a plate to that Mr. Drognag's room."

Horace brought some plates out and he and Putnam sat down to start their silent eating. Putnam thought about the new guest, who never left his room and said he had a few days to wait before opening his door. He noticed the flavors in his mouth weren't quite right.

"Where did you get this beef?"

"Not sure it's beef." Horace continued to eat but paused to try to pin down what sort of meat they were eating. "Horse, maybe?"

"I'll stick with the vegetables. From now on only beef or ham. Or chicken, or duck."

"What about fish or deer?"

"I think you get the gist. If you can't tell what it is, maybe skip it."

"Well, you know I'm half centaur, so what kind of meat never really matters to me."

"Half centaur? You're human."

"Exactly."

Putnam shot Horace a dirty look and went back to eating his potatoes and carrots and whatever else wasn't meat. He almost didn't notice the tiny old woman standing in the doorway.

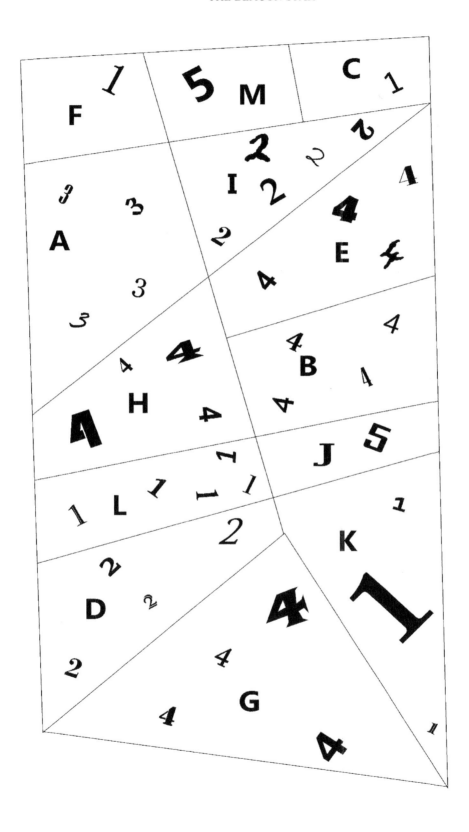

35

387

333

458

369

21

Junior was passsionate about the things he dreampt.

Senior was reaping what he sowed.

One was very vocal and said the things he meant.

One touched many people as he bowed.

With your back towards the mountains,

where their paths did cross,

Read between the names and in the notes.

Greatness comes in many forms and

sometimes it's our loss,

So heed the words surrounded by the quotes.

89

000001

329

175

The woman carefully stepped in and looked around. "I heard good things about this place." Her voice crackled with age but she did seem cheerful.

Standing up Putnam asked how he could be of service.

"I just need a room for a couple of nights. Maybe more, but just a couple for now."

Putnam went behind his counter and pulled out his ledger. "I have a very nice room for you, I'm sure you'll enjoy your stay."

The woman pulled a gold coin from her purse that Putnam didn't recognize and set it on the counter. Putnam pulled his box from under the counter, put the coin inside, and ran his check. When he was done he opened the box and looked back up at the old woman.

"This is alchemy. I generally don't take artificially created gold."

The old woman didn't miss a beat. "That's impressive, perhaps you care to barter?"

"I'm open to bartering."

"Well, I'm from the Crystal Mountains. As you know many a wizard and witch comes from there."

Putnam was aware of the mountains, named as they were full of crystals of every size and every kind. The very crystal that his money box worked from was from the Crystal mountains. But there was also much danger there. Several factions lay claims to the mountains and there was always a war going on somewhere.

The woman continued. "I came from West Easterham, it took me six months to get here."

"Easterham? Didn't you have to come through Sun Valley? That's guarded by the Gosns, they don't let anyone through."

"Indeed, unless they pay a toll. A little old woman on her own is no threat to those brutes, so they allowed me to speak, and I gave them gold."

Putnam shook his head and smiled. "Not the same you gave me? That's temporary, it'll turn back into lead or bronze or whatever it's made from."

"Yes, in a year, and it's been six months, so I must hurry back and go back through before that happens."

"But they're Gosns. They'll come after you, and your village, and anything in between. They won't like being made a fool of."

The old woman held up her hand. "They won't, I'll take care of that, you'll have to trust me." She paused and looked around as if she half expected a Gosn to jump out just then, but she continued. "Do you know the Velvet Door?"

Putnam did. It catered to kings and queens and anyone rich enough to afford their luxury. Most people couldn't afford to even be in the neighborhood where it stood, like a golden castle, above most of the city. "Yes," he said with a nod.

"Have you ever eaten there?"

Strange question but the answer was actually yes, many years ago at a function for innkeepers where standards and regulations were discussed. It was also a meeting where the Velvet Door could show off its offerings to every other innkeeper in the city. The food was, of course, top notch and some of the best he's ever tasted. "Yes, I wouldn't mind going back just for the food. It was delicious and savory and, well, I can't say enough about it."

"And how would you like to serve the same food here?"

Putnam shook his head. "Impossible. They have their own gardens and their own farms outside of the walls. They can afford runners to go further out. They have top notch chefs. Food is a huge part of their organization." He motioned to Horace, still sitting at the table dipping bread into his stew. "I have Horace and he's a good cook and we've never had a complaint about the food, but there's just no way I could make food like the Velvet Door."

The old woman leaned on the counter and motioned for Putnam to come closer. "Everything they make at the Velvet Door was taught to them by my grandmother. And I'll teach you. That's my barter. And you won't need anything that's not already in your kitchen. They don't want anyone to know that and all their gardens and runners are just for show. What do you say? You won't just be selling rooms but people will be showing up just to eat here and afford it without having to be a king."

In a low and careful voice Putnam asked, "I don't suppose you have any proof of all this?"

*****

Putnam pulled into his parking space and said hello to Tinker, who had been waiting longer than he wanted.

"Morning, Putnam. Ma'am."

Putnam still didn't care for Guild members but he had been hired by his guest. "Morning, Tinker. This is Kaloris."

"How do you do?" Tinker turned towards Putnam who was tending the horse. "Strange things are afoot. A zombie came up from the back way last night and never left."

This caught Putnam by surprise. Nothing can hurt anyone on the hill of course but zombies were smelly and messy and didn't have to hurt anyone to ruin your day. This was nothing compared to the next piece of news.

"There were some Gosns outside of the city. The guard that spotted them lost them in the dark, but there's no mistaking a Gosn, the big headless brutes. They didn't try to come in, though."

Putnam looked at old lady Kaloris, but she just shook her head. "It must be a coincidence. Come now, Mr. Tinker, let's get my grandmother's belongings and I'll sign my door back over to the Guild."

Leaning in close, Putnam whispered, "You aren't paying them with alchemist gold, are you? You can't fool the Guild."

"Don't worry, Mr. Putnam, my grandmother had her door in perpetuity, so signing it back over to the Guild more than covers any cost. Just get me home after and tonight I'll cook you a great big meal."

Tinker led Kaloris onto the path but turned one last time, smiled, then shouted "Beware of zombies!"

Putnam shuddered. He hated zombies but he feared Gosns more. They live right at the foot of the Crystal mountains but never could create magic and they resent it. This resentment is usually in the form of attacking and pillaging and extorting what they could out of anyone who crossed their path. Up to now they've always been distant stories to most in the town, but knowing some were outside the city walls was more than a coincidence. They were looking for trouble and trouble was staying at his inn.

*****

Hours later Putnam was pulling back into his inn with his old guest. The streets seemed deserted and many places were closed which was unusual for an early afternoon. He was surprised to see his own door closed with the shade drawn.

Horace met him in the yard before Putnam could even get off the wagon and led the horse into the stable and closed the gates and doors.

"Alright, what's going on?"

"There's a zombie wandering around. I could smell it earlier. If we're open we have to let it in."

Kaloris was helped out of the wagon and brushed herself off. "Zombies only do what they're told. It's not their fault they were reanimated."

"No, but that doesn't mean we have to like it. Here's your book and things."
Putnam handed Kaloris the small book she brought back along with a cloth sack

and he was dying to take a look into it, but he was still an innkeeper and respected the belongings of his guests.

As he led her inside she paused. "Isn't Horace coming in as well? He's the cook, he'll need to know these things."

"Well, he needs to stable the horse and take care of things."

"So he's going to take care of some horses then cook?"

"Well, he does wash in between."

"That's not the point, but I suppose we can wait."

"No, no, that's okay, the horses can wait a while."

Shrugging his shoulders Horace followed them into the inn.

*****

The meal was magnificent. She started out making a regular stew, almost a soup. She filled the kitchen with sweet smelling steam from the vegetables and even Horace's mystery meat. Then she opened the book and started a chant. She pulled a green crystal from her bag and waved it over the pot while turning pages and reading the chants. For a few moments she paused and had to read something twice, explaining that it's been decades since she's seen these spells and she wanted to get them just right. Then, declaring it was done she insisted they set the table in the dining room as if it were a fancy dinner.

Putnam didn't own many fancy dishes and what he did have didn't match, but what he had would do for a demonstration. He was still skeptical as the pot still looked like carrots and potatoes and chunks of meat like any other meal.

They set the table with a loaf of bread and set the forks and knives out like a proper meal.

"Now, magically changed food is still food. It will still fill you up, it will still keep you going, it will still be hot, the only difference being that we've changed the way it looks and tastes. If no one knows you didn't cook it, no one will care. They'll just think you are one hell of a cook." She winked at Horace. "Now, naturally you'd do this in the kitchen, where guests can't see."

She took the large ladle and scooped up the still steaming soup and poured it onto their plates. As she did, it swirled in different directions and formed a perfectly cooked steak and a bean salad, complete with a garnish and butter patty. The other plate turned out identical except this time the potato was covered in a pale gravy and on one corner of the plate a small chocolate formed. She set this plate in front of Horace.

"You see? It even knew your preferences. You'll each find your steak cooked exactly the way you like it. Other recipes can make chicken, or lamb, or duck, or whatever it is you decided to serve that day. All from a soup. Or stew, or anything really. Keep in mind they are eating the original food, it's just in a different form so you can't use anything spoiled."

After several bites Horace smiled and pointed at the book. "Would you mind if I had a gander?"

Kaloris nodded and Horace eagerly started flipping through the pages. "And I don't have to be a wizard? These spells will work?"

"With the crystal. The greener the better. But don't let on, otherwise people will only see it as novelty food, not as fine food as they have at the Velvet Door."

They were interrupted by a slow, heavy knock at the door but with the shades drawn they couldn't see who it was.

Kaloris snatched the book out of Horace's hand and tucked it under her arm then grabbed the pot. "We mustn't let anyone see this. I'll take care of it in the kitchen while you tend to your visitor."

After she shuffled through the kitchen door Putnam answered the door and shocked to see two Gosns, with swords and spears, standing in his entry way. Their faces and ears were on their chests making them look like huge, headless barbarians. Standing in the street behind them were two city guards, watching them closely.

"Can I help you…" Putnam started, but was interrupted.

"We're looking for an old woman. And a book. We heard she was staying here."

Putnam looked between them at the guards and Horace came up and stood behind him. "Now look, I don't want any trouble and the city is under the protection of the hill…"

"Oh, there won't be no trouble." The Gosn's voice was thin and raspy. "We just want a peaceful visit with the old woman. If she refuses our request we'll leave peacefully." The way he spoke sounded as if leaving peacefully was the last thing on his mind.

The guards could hear everything and one nodded at Putnam. "We'll be right here, sir." Whether he was talking to Putnam or the Gosns wasn't clear.

The protection spell did protect anyone in the city from physical harm and if a fight was started the spell manifested in different ways to stop it. Sometimes freezing the aggressor, sometimes causing people to fall into a trance and separating, and sometimes just causing people to forget what was going on but Putnam knew it didn't stop foul language, or threats, or even stand offs if neither party was attacking. If he attacked the Gosns he knew it would be a mark against his inn so if anything, he had to make sure no matter what happened the Gosns had to make the first move.

And he would leave the door open so the guards would be witness to anything that happened.

Kaloris came in from the kitchen wiping her hands, which were stained with something brownish red. Putnam only momentarily tried to figure out what she could have been doing to cause that.

"Now then," she said, "What's all this about?"

One of the Gosns took a menacing step forward. "You stole a book from us, and we're here to get it back."

What fresh hell is this? Putnam thought.

The other Gosn stepped forward as well, prompting the guards to step through the door. "And we're willing to tear this place apart to find it."

"Um." Putnam stuck up his finger. "I will object to that."

The guards stepped around the Gosns and stood between them and Kaloris. With all this muscle in his dining room Putnam realized that it was smaller than he thought.

"Let's all just calm down here." The taller guard decided to take charge of this situation. "You claim she stole a book from you? How so?"

The Gosns exchanged glances. "Well, not from us, exactly. From our grandparents. We've been trying to find it for decades. We heard she pulled it out of a door just this morning and we can prove it's ours. Inside the cover is our grandfather's writing, dedicating it to his favorite wife."

The guard turned to Putnam. "Is this true? Did you see her with a book?"

The room seemed to spin just a tiny bit. Putnam hated confrontation of any kind and now he was right in the thick of it. "As you know," he started, with his voice shaking just a little bit, "I am an innkeeper who caters to openers, and I am bound by Sugar Hill and Crescent City to keep their private matters private." He wasn't sure if this was the correct card to play but it cleared him from the whole situation.

The guard nodded a nod of annoyance and said, "Is that so?" He turned to the other guard. "Let's just take them all before a magistrate and get this sorted out."

One of the Gosns held up a hand. "If we leave that will give someone the chance to come in and take the book, which she obviously hid, we would like to handle things right here."

"Alright, if that's how you want to play it, we'll bring the magistrate here, for now everyone sit at a table where I can keep an eye on you." He sent the other guard out who blew a few notes on a horn which were answered with another far away

362

38

∧

95

1
Columbus ever pointing
but which way to go?
Down the beaten war path and
the bronco busta show.
If you reach the halls of knowledge
then you've gone too far.
Return back to the arches
where the pillars are.
Across the promenade two kings
exchange a stare.
Words are written twice but
only read once there.

262

184

241

000010

204

289

horn. He blew a few more and was answered again, it was the secret language of the guards.

Everyone reluctantly sat down except Putnam who began to gather the plates up, if there was a dispute about the book he didn't want two perfectly cooked steaks laying about to prove it was here. "I'll just clean this up…"

"No." One of the Gosns slapped the table. "Nothing moves. If that book is here it stays where it is until we find it."

The guard nodded.

Putnam sat down next to Horace who was wide eyed and afraid to move.

It was the most tense hour of Putnam's life waiting for a magistrate to appear. When he did finally show up he brought 4 more guards with him. He was little man, old beyond his years, dressed in red robes and silken shorts. "This had better be good."

Before anyone could speak he held up his hand which silenced everyone whether they wanted to be silenced or not. He then pulled a small candle from one of his deep pockets and plopped it on the table.

It lit by itself.

"Okay," he began, "I will hear all sides and all will tell the truth. If you lie, the candle will flicker. What I decide will be final and all parties will agree to my decisions. If anyone objects to this speak now."

Everyone just stared at the candle.

"I know Gosns may not be familiar with the ways of our city, do you have any questions?"

"We are, in fact, familiar with the ways of your city and will abide by its rules as we know we are in the right." The Gosn said all of that through clenched teeth. "In spite of what you think we are an honorable people who protect a large part of the mountains. We stick our necks out for many a village."

Horace choked back a laugh.

"I heard what I said. We are a proud people and hold our heads high."

Again Horace choked back an even bigger laugh.

"I heard what I said. In any case, we know we're in the right and will abide by this magistrate."

"I agree." Said Kaloris, putting her nose in the air.

In the next hour the Gosns explained how their grandfather's book was stolen ages ago and they pretty much know who did it so when the granddaughter of the thief came through their village they knew if they followed her she would lead them to the book. They even wrote, directly on Putnam's table, what would be inscribed inside the cover. That would prove their story true.

Kaloris produced a bag of crystals and dumped them on the table stating that it was these which she pulled from the door this morning. Her grandmother's best. Putnam was amazed when the candle didn't flicker until he realized that technically she was telling the truth, she did pull those from the door. She just didn't mention that she pulled something else with them.

The Gosns then insisted that every inch of the inn be searched which Putnam had to protest. He did, after all, have a guest that wouldn't leave his room and as an innkeeper the guests were his number one priority.

The magistrate took all of this in and only had to think for a few moments.

"I will grant the search, one Gosn and one guard will do a tidy search of any area the Gosn sees fit. I will grant Mr. Putnam a written statement saying it was on my orders to clear his inn of any responsibility."

Kaloris stood up, and tapped the table. "If this inn is to be searched then I suggest it's only fair to have the Gosns empty all their belongings onto the table first, to be sure they don't plant anything."

The magistrate nodded. "So granted. Now, if no book is found all parties will leave peacefully. If a book is indeed found with their inscription, it shall be turned over to the Gosns. If it does not contain the inscription it shall become the property of Miss Kaloris. Are we in full agreement?"

For a long moment everyone exchanged glances as if they were reading each other's mind.

Then, without any prompting, the Gosns began to empty their pockets onto the table. There were knives and swords and other weapons but there was also things any traveler would have like cooking tongs, string, rags, flints, and little boxes. Lastly, they each laid down a small sack of gold coins. The magistrate ordered two of the guards to watch their things.

Putnam didn't like it but one guard and one Gosn set about searching the inn, starting in the kitchen. The magistrate followed them.

Kaloris nudged Putnam.

"What?" he said, annoyed that she would bring such chaos into his peaceful domain.

She raised her eyebrows and nodded at the sacks of gold. Then she did it again.

He looked but didn't know what she wanted him to see. She cleared her throat while whispering, "Velvet Door."

He looked again then he saw it. There was a small crest on each bag, the crest of the Velvet Door.

"Someone sent them to protect someone's interest, methinks." She said calmly, trying not to attract the attention of the remaining guards.

"Is what they said true?"

"My grandmother was no thief. She told me she bought the book."

"With alchemist gold?"

This seemed to strike a nerve with Kaloris. "Regardless, the Velvet Door sent them, paid them to get the book, so no one would know their secret."

"Maybe."

Putnam sat back and waited.

*****

It was dusk when the search was finally over. The magistrate and the guards were clearly tired and a small crowd had formed outside trying to figure out what was going on in the Beacon Star. Putnam was hoping this didn't damage his reputation too much but having ruffians and guards in your inn was never a good sign.

The magistrate took a deep breath and faced the Gosns. "Are you satisfied that no book is on the premises at all?"

"No. But if she leaves the city right now we won't press the issue."

Before the magistrate could speak Kaloris spoke up. "I'll agree to that. My things are already packed and well searched. I'll leave right now."

The magistrate raised his eyebrows. "So be it. It is dark, are you sure you won't wait until morning?"

"I've been in the wilderness for six months, I can handle myself. Horace, will you fetch my bag, maybe a Gosn can go with you to make sure nothing is afoot." There was a balance of sarcasm and contempt in her voice.

A Gosn did indeed follow Horace to her room where he fetched her bag. She threw it over her shoulder and with three of the guards in tow headed to the city gates. The Gosns insisted they had already made arrangements for the night and were allowed to go, although they followed Kaloris to the gates first, with their own set of guards.

Putnam gave the magistrate a gold coin from his own coffer which was customary in such situations and finally he and Horace sat down to the now ice cold plates.

Horace jumped right back up. "The poor horse has been bridled all this time, I'm sure he hates me right now." He ran out through the back door.

Putnam sat reflecting on the day. If the Velvet Door did indeed use the book to make all their food then they'd stop at nothing to protect that secret. And when two Gosns wandered into the city who better to retrieve it for them? He would, of course, keep all this a secret. He may need a favor from the Velvet Door one day and this was just the leverage he'd need to call on that favor.

The only thing he couldn't figure out was what happened to the book.

Just then Horace came back in shaking his head. "It reeks out there, and the door was unlatched. I think that damned zombie was in our stable. There was goo on the floor."

Putnam started laughing.

"What on earth is so funny? This was the worst day in all my years here."

"That's where the book went. She probably jammed it up inside the zombie's rib cage. It's gonna wander back out the back way and she'll meet up with it somewhere. That's what was on her fingers when she came back from the kitchen. That's why she filled the kitchen with steam, so we wouldn't smell it. She had everything planned out from the start, right down to stiffing me on her bill."

"Well, not exactly." Horace pulled a folded up piece of paper out of his pocket. "This page fell out of the book when I was looking at it. I hid it before anyone saw. From what I can tell it's a cake recipe and all we need is a green crystal."

Putnam kept laughing. "Well, let's borrow a green crystal from somewhere and see if it works."

The next day Putnam and Horace had the best cake either had ever tasted and they invited their neighbors on the street in for some. His reputation, if it was ever in jeopardy, was restored and there were already inquiries for how much it would cost for him to bake more cakes.

While cleaning Kaloris's room later that day he found a note on the wash basin.

"Thanks for everything. Enjoy the cake."

Putnam smiled.

She really did plan everything.

III. The Golden Ratio

Putnam tied a small sack of potatoes to a hook on an old saddle. "Are you sure you won't stay just one more night? It's nearly nightfall already, you won't make it too far."

The short squat man who had been staying at the inn for the last two days just shook his head and climbed into the saddle. His even smaller wife climbed up behind him.

"Have you forgotten we live underground? We can see where you surface dwellers cannot. The night hides nothing from us. Thank you very much Mr. Putnam, you have been most helpful, but we must get this cure back to our people before anyone else succumbs to the illness."

"I understand. May luck go with you."

The man tipped his hat and with a gentle nudge rode his horse out of the courtyard. Horace swung the gate closed and leaned his cheek on a fence post. He watched as the riders turned the corner to the main gate.

"Something wrong, Horace?" Putnam said, himself leaning on the gate to see what Horace was looking at.

"Nah, not really." Putnam stayed where he was, seemingly waiting, so Horace went on. "Well, it's just that when their people write the story of this adventure it will state that the heroes stayed at an inn in the city, then continued on their way. And that guy getting the spear of destiny or whatever it was called, stayed at an inn. And those people trying to rescue their king, stayed at an inn. Sometimes I feel like I'd like more than a sentence in some adventure story."

"Ah, but who wants to read that their heroes ate pork and bread, drank some mead, drunkenly courted a woman in the street, then snored for a few hours before scratching their head at ten thousand doors before finding what they need to complete their quest? It's just a boring, mundane, unflattering detail that is best left out."

After a few moments he added, "Besides, things do happen in inns. They meet their contacts, they devise their plans. Sometimes they have an epiphany. Or meet their soul mate. Or, heaven forbid, get poisoned. If there's a detail it'll get written into the story."

Horace stood up and looked back over the courtyard. "Oh, don't get me wrong, I'm quite happy here. It's not strenuous work by any means. You not only pay well but you're a good friend, and I get to meet people from all races, from all over. It's a pretty good life. I just wouldn't mind leaving a legacy somehow. But don't fret, I'll think of something."

Putnam stayed by the gate and waved at a few people passing by. It was dinner time and things were always quiet this time of night. Just as he was about to return to his evening chores a couple of constables walked up, tipping their hats.

"Mr. Putnam, may we have a word inside?"

Horace was just cleaning a table when he saw Putnam and the constables enter and without a word served up some mugs of beer. This was, overall, a peaceful city but the peacekeepers were still respected and it was customary to offer them drinks should they visit your establishment.

"We're just here to ask a few questions, Mr. Putnam. It seems a few things have gone missing." The constable looked tired and a bit tipsy, he had obviously been visiting many establishments. His partner continued drinking so he went on.

"A certain comb came up missing at one of the inns. A small matter although it was expensive and inlaid with gold. As a matter of duty we questioned the neighboring shops and found they each claimed some things were missing. Small things. Things so small they didn't care or just thought they lost."

"What sort of things?"

The constable shrugged. "A small box, a bag of carrots, a hat..."

"A chair." the other constable offered.

"Yes, a chair. So the magistrate has ordered an investigation to see if there's any sort of pattern. Just because the whole thing is weird."

The other constable nodded. "Yes, we have orders to ask everyone if anything, no matter how small, is missing."

Putnam thought for a moment then looked up at Horace.

"Well, now that you mention it," said Horace, "We're missing a pitchfork. We had three and one day there was two. I did look around and couldn't find it anywhere. I even asked the neighbors if they borrowed it. It's just a pitchfork so I didn't think much of it until now."

One off the constables pulled a scroll off his belt and unrolled slightly and to the long list already there added The Beacon Star: Pitchfork.

"Do you have any guests? We have to ask them the same."

"At the moment we have just two. A Miss Swedit, she's scheduled for two days, just came in today. I'm taking her to the hill in the morning. And a Mr. Swagurei. But we can't disturb him."

The constable raised an eyebrow. "And why not?"

3	0	9	4	7	9	4	4	6	5	1	5	2	3
1	1	1	1	0	3	5	9	1	7	1	2	1	3
8	2	2	8	3	9	9	0	8	5	5	6	5	1
7	1	4	3	4	8	9	7	3	3	4	0	1	9
8	6	7	0	X	3	X	2	X	3	3	6	8	6
9	2	0	X	5	R	E	A	D	X	1	1	0	7
6	0	9	1	X	C	L	U	E	X	9	3	2	1
4	1	1	X	9	F	R	O	M	X	0	2	4	4
9	3	3	4	X	E	A	C	H	X	7	1	3	0
7	7	4	X	4	X	0	X	1	X	4	3	9	6
3	8	4	8	0	2	3	5	7	9	4	0	9	5
9	9	0	2	4	0	0	1	0	6	5	9	6	1
2	4	3	0	0	1	8	3	3	3	7	0	6	0
4	1	0	9	1	1	3	7	0	9	3	3	1	5

184

256

357

313

189

8

Cross Simms and Kipling, Car, Allison,

Wadsworth and then Sheridan.

Near beer and water, cars and bend,

A pretty place is where you'll end.

The place where this one calls home.

But back up and telephone,

123

000011

362

317

"Well, I'm not sure what race he is, but he comes from the far south. Some wintry place. All he does is sleep, for months at a time. If we wake him he can become, um, unpleasant. We've taken every care not to disturb him."

The constables exchanged glances. "That," one said, "is the very definition of suspicious. We're going to have to wake him. We have our orders."

Moments later Putnam was nervously knocking on Mr. Swagurei's door. Then he knocked again.

And again.

The constables were getting impatient but Putnam told them it might be a while.

"Don't you have a key?"

"Of course, but he's a paying guest in good standing and as far as I know he's done nothing wrong. Just a few more." He knocked again.

Just before he was about to knock again the door jiggled a bit then opened. And old, skinny man with vaguely elvish features opened the door. His deeply sunken eyes were all black and under his sleeves his arms bent as if they had an extra elbow somewhere.

"How can anyone sleep if you keep interrupting them?"

Putnam cleared his throat. "Sir it's been a while since…"

"You woke me up just two months ago."

"Your bed was on fire."

"It would have sorted itself out eventually. What's on fire this time?"

"Ahem." The constables stepped forward. "We need to ask you a few questions."

The old man eyed them up and down. "Well, ask."

"Is anything missing out of your room?"

Mr. Swagurei's mouth frowned and his eyes arched at the same time. He seemed to be too angry to speak and when he finally did it was restrained and cracking. "Is that all you wanted? You woke me up for that?"

The constables were unphased. "Is anything missing?"

After scowling a moment and without leaving the doorway the man turned around, looked left and right, then turned back towards the constables.

"My belt is missing."

Everyone raised their eyebrows in surprise. "Are you sure?"

"Yes, I'm sure. It was still on my pants when I laid down, ain't there now."

One of the constables leaned into the doorway and could see a beltless pair of pants hanging over a chair. Mr. Swagurei never moved. The constable shrugged and pulled out his scroll.

"Can I go back to sleep now?"

Putnam nodded. "Yes, I'll try not to...." He was interrupted by the slamming door.

He turned toward the constables. "That," he said, "Was unexpected."

Weeks later Putnam had forgotten all about the constables and was sitting by the bar with a guest just chatting. This man was from a place with strange animals and was giving a description of each while Putnam polished a few beer steins. Horace was picking up dinner dishes and humming to himself when all of sudden a large deafening pop filled the room.

Everyone froze.

"Which one was that, then?" Horace asked, eyes wide.

"Princess Gergely."

The two men stared at each other for a moment. The lone guest looked back and forth between them wondering what in the world was going on.

Putnum started tapping the counter with a quick, nervous tap. "Um, what are we low on? We need hay and feed, we have a large stable and we can use that. Also stuff for cake. And we'll need to clear all the rooms."

Horace crossed the room and headed towards the back door through the kitchen. "I'll get the stables ready, order the hay before anyone else can, and on the way back I'll get some meat and fresh veggies."

"Beef!" Putnam shouted after him. "Make sure you know it's beef."

Putnam noticed his wide eyed guest. "Oh, nothing to be worried about, Mr. Bendy. The city sometimes gets huge guests. Kings and queens, and sometimes princesses. Usually we get advanced notice but sometimes they show up unannounced. Normally it doesn't concern us as they stay in palaces on the other side of town but sometimes they show up with huge entourages, servants, butlers, mistresses, stable boys. So we get all the overflow. The thing is, they usually send a runner ahead to let us know."

He leaned in and lowered his voice. "Sometimes they show up, out of the blue, and bleed us dry as we can't get supplies fast enough. About twenty years ago an innkeeper stumbled upon a doorbell spell. It gives us advanced warning when nothing else does. There's about twenty of us with this spell, it gives us just a bit of an edge. They'll all come by later and we'll plan out accommodations."

Mr. Bendy leaned in, still a little wide eyed. "Is that above board?"

Looking around and leaning forward, in spite of the fact they were alone, Putnam said, "Well, we do try to be fair, but many inns were offered the spell and turned it down. Although more buy in with each visit. Every time it's used, you see, it costs us a gold coin. Not much considering the return but some still balk at it. We do keep it hidden, though, mine is that portrait on the wall." He pointed to a painting of what looked like three musicians gathered by a lake. "That bass drum pops it skin, that's what you heard. Everyone has their own warning. No one's the wiser."

"Do you ever get nobility staying here, Mr. Putnam?"

He smiled a broad smile. "All my guests are royalty, Mr. Bendy. All my guests are royalty."

*****

After two hours of cleaning the main entrance, Putnam felt like something was off, but he couldn't quite put his finger on it. Outside a wagon went by, with three passengers, as darkness started to fill the streets and lanterns lit up like random fireflies.

Across the street he could see the familiar faces in the Singing Robin drinking beer and shouting at each other. The place was always a mess in the morning. He would have thought that old Beale, the proprietor, would be cleaning as much the Beacon Star was being cleaned.

So why wasn't he?

Putnam put down his rag and walked across the street. All the inns and pubs on the street had good camaraderie and looked out for each other so it seemed right that Putnam should check to see if Beale's doorbell spell had gone off.

A few moments later he was back in the street wondering why it hadn't. Looking up the street he could see Aurora shaking out a rug while yelling orders back through the door. It seemed she had gotten the notice.

At that moment Horace came trumbling down the street and waved as he hopped off the cart and opened the gate. "Got some good bargains, Mr. Putnam, late in the day, no one buying. We'll have hay and feed delivered at sunrise. Will fill us up plus some."

"Horace," Putnam asked, as he walked through the gate with the cart, "were there others in the market stocking up?"

"Well, Mayfair's group was there. I was the only one ordering feed. You'd think there'd be a run on supplies, but there wasn't."

"The Singing Robin's doorbell was missing. He had a chair that would hop around, it wasn't to be found anywhere."

Putnam patted the pony pulling the cart. In the distance the town clock was chiming. "Horace, do you know all twelve of the people who bought doorbell spells?"

"I do. But there's way more than twelve."

"Twelve with Gergely spells, that I know of. I'll take care of this, you go to all twelve and tell them there's an important meeting here, at six bells. We need to find out if the princess is coming or not."

*****

The next morning, as the sun was rising and the town clock was striking the hour, Putnam's dining hall filled up with curious innkeepers. Some thought they would be discussing the big event but some had no idea why they had been summoned.

Putnam wasted no time and once he had everyone's attention he asked who had their doorbells go off.

Only a few had.

This excited the small crowd and voices were asking, "Is Princess Gergely coming or not?"

"The real question is, why didn't some of our doorbells go off?"

"It's not that mine didn't go off, it's missing altogether." shouted the owner of the Prancing Turtle.

With that, half the people went silent. "That's odd, mine was missing as well."

"As was mine."

"Mine was home, and certainly went off. It was a pitchfork and the tines were ringing like bells."

Horace nudged Putnam. "We had a pitchfork stolen a while back." A couple puzzle pieces snapped together in Putnam's mind. "Aurora, did you have anything stolen a while back, I remember the constables made a round."

Aurora thought for a moment. "Yes, I had a painting taken from the hallway. A crappy one if I recall."

"Okay, you, Mr. Mayfair. Your doorbell went off, what was it?"

"Mine was a vase, threw flowers in the air."

From across the room someone said, "I had a vase stolen."

Putnam zeroed in on the voice. "And I'll wager that whatever you had as a doorbell, Mr. Mayfair was missing."

"Mine was a small box. With a brass inlay."

Mr. Mayfair started shaking his head. "Aye, I did have a box stolen. Just my recipe box. It was empty at the time."

Putnam smiled the smile of someone who had figured something out that no one else could. "Someone was trying to steal back all the doorbells. They just got their list mixed up. So I think the princess is coming but someone doesn't want anyone to know."

"But who would do such a thing?"

"Could be another inn."

"Or, Princess Gergely. All the spells were tied to her, my Prince Ricardlessly spell didn't go off, and wasn't stolen. I wonder if she is traveling incognito and doesn't want anyone to know."

"But even she wouldn't know about her doorbell spell. What royalty would?."

"Well, someone knows about these spells and doesn't want them to go off. I guess we need to see if she arrives today, and with how many people, and who benefits the most from her arrival."

The meeting broke up after some banter as everyone had guests to attend to and supplies to get, just in case. Outside some wagons were already heading towards the hill, filled with guests. He hated to do it but Putnam flagged down one of the wagons and asked a favor of its driver.

If anyone knew a princess was coming, it would be The Guild.

*****

"Good afternoon, Mr. Putnam."

"Good afternoon, Mr. Tinker."

Putnam hated the Guild and disliked Tinker but of all the Guild members he was the one he trusted. He kept his word and understood that allies were valuable so didn't mind bending the rules a little bit to keep relationships open.

The two men sat at a table in front of the window where they could see people passing by. Putnam idly tapped a gold coin on the table top while he talked.

"I need some information, officially. I know the Guild keeps tabs on just about every king and queen and prince and princess in all the realms. And I would like to know if any are on their way to the city."

"Anyone in particular?" Tinker tried not to look at the gold coin.

"I'm sure the Guild is aware that some inns have doorbell spells."

"Well, they are frowned upon, but personally I don't see the harm."

Putnam leaned in. "A few months ago there was a rash of thefts of common items. Items that no real thief would ever care about. It turns out they were trying to steal doorbell spells. They didn't get them all, including mine."

Tinker's ears perked up. "That is indeed interesting, especially since there are no royal visitors expected. And that's the Guild's official word. Who's doorbell went off, if you don't mind my asking?"

"Well, what can you tell me about Princess Gergely?"

Tinker thought for a bit. "Friend of the city, good trade relations with their neighbors, kingdom is very peaceful. Very wealthy, generous but not too generous. All around nothing bad to say."

"So, why would someone try to steal all her doorbells?"

"I can tell you this, Mr. Putnam, her door is a very prominent one. She won't be opening it without attracting a lot of attention. And most royalty have no ideas about doorbells and don't care. And she has body guards and servants, if she was traveling towards the city everyone would know it so hiding, or stealing, the doorbells would have little effect over all. But still, this is very interesting information. I'm not sure what to make of it." He finally looked down at the gold coin. "I do consider this exchange of information beneficial, Mr. Putnam. If someone is trying to hide the visit of a royal, the Guild would like to know. And I'm sure you heard what you wanted in knowing we have no information ourselves of a royal visit. Is there anything else you be wanting?"

Putnam thought for a bit. "Not really, Mr. Tinker. If you think we're even, then we're even. And I do appreciate it. Is the Guild still supporting refugees on the east side?"

"We are. Unofficially of course."

"Then consider this an unofficial donation." He rolled the coin across the table and Tinker caught it before it could fall over. It was Putnam's way of paying for information without actually paying for information. He honestly thought Tinker would charge him but was happy with how things turned out.

After some tea, Tinker had to take his leave. As he was walking out he turned back towards Putnam. "Mr. Putnam, if the princess does show up, it might be in

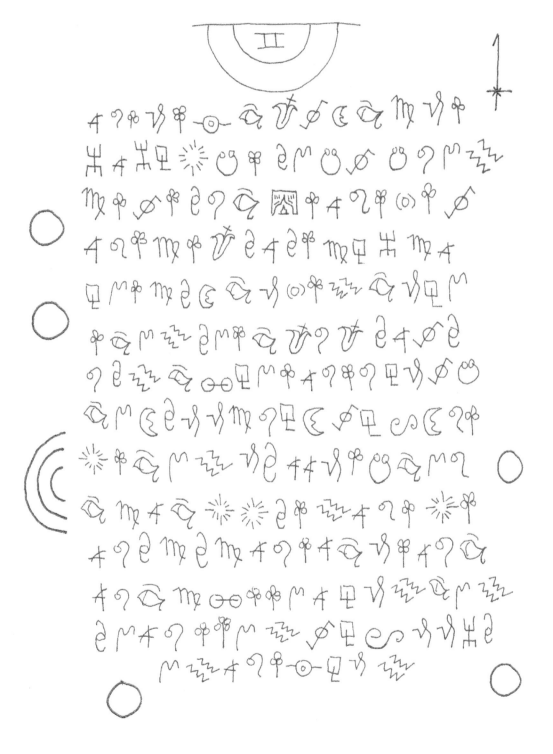

128

390

∧ ∧

27

3

Of the many things you'll climb,

Mountains, stairs, and history.

164

On the crumbling stones you'll find,

466

446

The beginnings of a mystery.

From Mummy Ridge to Pike's Peak,

Many things were written fast.

But in time's shadow is where to sneak,

To read this clue's explosive past.

000101

322

134

everyone's best interest if the Guild knew. We do have bigger pieces of the overall picture of things and something like that may prove to be valuable information."

Putnam smiled. "I'll be sure to mention it if I hear anything."

The next day all questions were answered when a hooded figure came into the Beacon Star. She threw back her hood to reveal perfectly kept hair and her green eyes looked as if they were carved from emeralds. When she spoke her voice was perfectly smooth and every word sounded as if it were pulled from a song.

"Sorry about the smell, I stepped in some droppings earlier."

Putnam stood tall behind the desk. "How may we be of service?"

"I need a room for a few weeks." She pulled a pouch from under her cloak and dumped out some huge silver coins. "I see you have a room that overlooks the street, is that available?"

Putnam pointed to the ceiling. "We do but it's right over the dining area so it's not quiet at times."

"It will be perfectly ok."

After showing her to her room and explaining his services Putnam went out to the stables to find Horace. Horace wasn't even able to say hello when he was dragged to the back stall.

"She's here," Putnam said excitedly, but still able to whisper. "Princess Gergely is here. Incongnito. Said her name was Cynthia."

Horace just stared, "Are you sure it's her?"

Putnam acted like he was just asked if water is wet. "Well yes. She's gorgeous. She was wearing silk clothes and had a woolen cloak. And she paid with silver from the Duchy of Ven."

Horace kept staring. "Are you sure it's her? We get lots of silver."

"Look," Putnam started counting on his fingers. "First of all there are only two ways to get here from her kingdom, go north and take the Seventy Year Pass or head east and come up the roads where the plains meets the mountains. So think about this logically. She's a princess and while the Seventy Year Pass is relatively safe it's sparse. Not many inns and villages, you would have to camp half the time. A princess just wouldn't do that. Now, if you came up the roads where the plains meets the mountains there are towns and cities and the Duchy of Ven, a princess can travel in style. And the Duchy is on a silver standard so you'd end up with silver coins."

"But are you sure it's her?"

"Well, there was a tag on her bag that said Gergely."

"You know, you could have led with that."

"Then you'd just think she was a royal servant or something, with a bag from the house of Gergely."

"Hadn't thought of that. I think that now."

Putnam stared at the ground. "I wonder why she's here. I wonder why someone tried to steal the doorbell spells."

"You are missing a major point here."

"What?"

"The whole point of the doorbell spells is so we can prepare for a royal entourage. And there isn't one, so no one is going to make any money."

"I wonder if I should tell the inns."

"No, if she is the princess…"

"…Which she is…"

"…Which she may not be, but if she is then she went through a lot of trouble to hide her arrival. We should respect that."

"Not too much trouble. Whoever tried to steal the doorbell spells wasn't very competent, and she's not hiding her expensive clothes or pampered looks. And tomorrow when she walks up to open a royal door on the hill every guild member and luxury innkeeper will come running."

"Speaking of which, one of us had better get back to the front. She may have been followed, or have body guards or something that will show up. And if some random Guild members show up then we'll know that they know."

"Good thinking. And make a good meal tonight, but don't make it look like you are trying to make it special."

"Isn't that what I always do?"

That night at dinner Putnam sat across from Horace at one table while their two guests sat at another. There were a few locals at the third table and they were drinking and laughing to themselves.

Putnam leaned into the table and whispered hard at Horace. "Rabbit? Where did you get rabbits?"

"The Gergely Kingdom is known for rabbits, I just wanted to show off my recipie."

"We're trying not to look suspicious."

"Then why did you open that wine from Troid? That bottle cost more than our wagon and all our ponies together."

"I just felt like a good wine tonight."

"And I just felt like a little rabbit."

As if on queue the locals raised their glasses towards Horace. "You outdid yourself tonight, Horace." shouted one slightly drunk guest. "I could live on these for a month."

"Hear, hear." shouted Mr. Crisswell, the other guest staying that night.

The room went quiet and everyone turned towards Cynthia. She paused mid bite when she finally noticed. "Um, yes, quite good."

Everyone cheered again then went back to their meals. Later, when Horace was picking up plates full of bones and silverware Cynthia moved over to Putnam's table.

"That was a very good meal, Mr. Putnam, and the wine was excellent."

"Thank you, Miss Cynthia. I'll pass it along to Horace. He's quite skilled." He tried not to think of the fact that he was sitting next to a real life princess who just paid him a compliment here in his humble inn.

"I was wondering if I may ask you something, about the symbol on your door frame."

"Of course."

She pulled out an old parchment and carefully unrolled it on the table. It had strange symbols scattered about and she pointed to one in the lower corner, a tall, thin triangle with 4 lines coming out of its apex.

Putnam squinted at it. "That's the beacon."

"Does it mean anything, it's missing the star that you have. Can it be found anywhere else in town?"

"Well, when I bought the inn, oh, several decades ago now, it was just called Hillside. I thought that was rather uninspired. This symbol was indeed on the door frame and I thought it looked like a beacon. I added the star myself and thus we became the Beacon Star. May I ask what this is all about?"

"This is a type of walking map, used by older generations back in my...um, where I'm from. I'm supposed to start at this symbol and head in this direction until I see this symbol, turn left until I see this symbol, and so on. Do either of these look familiar to you?"

"They do indeed. I see them almost every single day. This one is on a large paving stone in the middle of an intersection just down the street. This one is on the gate, on the side of the hill. Well, the wall next to where the gate used to be. They are in almost a straight line from one another. Clever thing, this walking map, but it must have been made before my time if the star isn't there."

"It's centuries old."

Putnam raised an eyebrow. "Hmm, this inn was only a couple decades old when I took over. Not sure what was here before. Either that symbol was on what was here before or someone was a good guesser. It does fit in with the intersection and the gate, though."

Cynthia thought for a moment or two.

"When I take you to the hill in the morning I can show you both."

"I'll see you in the morning, Mr. Putnam.

After she was gone Putnam picked up some of the remaining plates and took them to the kitchen where Horace was busy cleaning. "I hate to say this, but for the second time in as many days I need to speak to Tinker. When we get to the hill in morning we need to make sure we find him."

The next morning on the trip to the hill Putnam pointed out the design in the bricks at the intersection. Parts had been repaired over the years so there were different textures and colors but the design was basically the same. As they rounded the corner and grew closer to the hill he pointed out the spot on the wall with the next symbol. They couldn't drive straight for it, though, as there were now fences and parking in the fields around the hill.

Putnam pulled into his parking space and pointed towards the main gate. "All the royal doors are in that direction." he said without thinking.

"Why would I want to go to the royal doors?" Cynthia said.

"Oh, um, no reason, they are just very ornate and beautiful if you find yourself in that direction." He walked her to the fence and showed her the third symbol, almost rubbed away from the stone it was carved in so long ago.

"You know," started Putnam, "I've never really thought about these symbols, they are all over town and the hill when you think about it."

"And I have a lot more to find, but I think I'll carry on on my own." She smiled a perfect smile and headed up the hill.

Reluctantly, Putnam returned to his wagon where Horace was taking care of the ponies and chatting with Tinker.

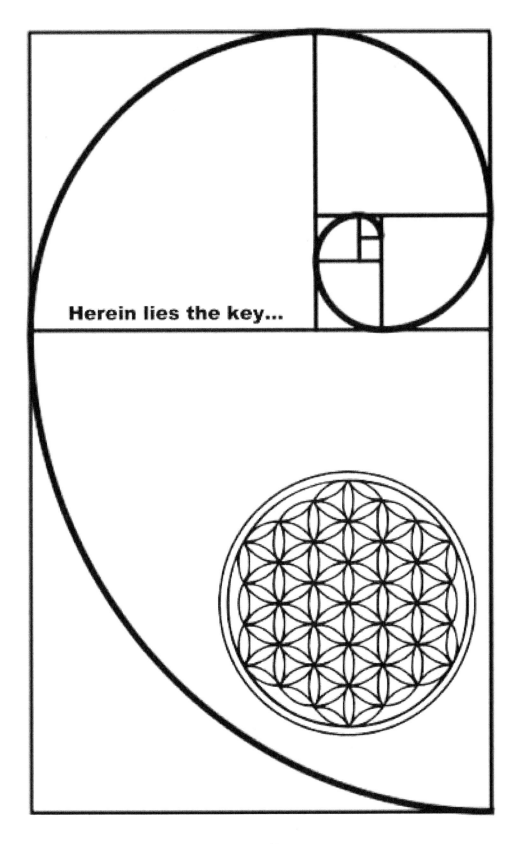

Herein lies the key...

215

454

∧

334

191

85

152

2

Beneath the dome of gold do go,
Then head down stairs long and steep.
To the obelisk below,
Where five seals we do keep.
The first eight you'll read and then,
Take a knee and shed a tear.
Dedicated to great men,
Whose memories do linger here.

001000

173

233

"I found Tinker for you, and I'm off to pay our fees for the month." Horace knew Putnam wanted some privacy.

Putnam swore to himself that he'd never tell but he just had to tell someone. "I just led Princess Gergely to the hill."

Tinker's eyes grew wide. "Are you sure? We had no idea any royal was in town."

"Well, she calls herself Cynthia but she has the royal emblem on everything and is perfect in every way, so..." he shrugged. Before Tinker could speak he added, "But she's incognito. I don't think we should tell anyone else."

"The Guild has to know, if nothing else they'll discreetly increase security around your place. We don't have to tell the guards what for. I will only bring it up with the elders, for information purposes."

Putnam grew defensive. "Look, I don't want The Guild to do anything drastic. She obviously doesn't want anyone to know, I'm already regretting telling you this."

"So why did you?"

"Because she's a princess, staying at my place, I had to tell someone. Also, she has something called a walking map. She said it's centuries old but it starts at the Beacon Star, only it wasn't the Beacon Star when it was made. Can you look in the historical records to see what stood in it's spot before?"

Putnam explained the walking map and how it matched the symbol on his door. Tinker looked up the hill and could just make out the princess walking amongst the doors.

"The Guild will need payment for the record search or they'll know something's up. A couple of silver. I should get back, I'm nervous about her walking around up there, all by herself. She may be safe from harm but someone could still take advantage of her. We'll just make sure some patrols just happen to be walking her way is all."

"It shouldn't go any farther than that, if word gets out my place will be mobbed, and who knows what else. Can you come by tonight?" He handed Tinker a couple of silver coins.

"I should be able to search the records by then. I'll ask in passing if anyone has heard of a walking map as well, or if anyone has ever wondered about symbols around town. Many intersections are decorated, and many walls have carvings, but I would have never put a purpose to them any more than decoration before now."

Tinker turned to leave but Putnam stopped him. "Tinker, I trust you."

"I know, Mr. Putnam," he said nodding. "Believe me, it's not all about making money with The Guild, sometimes it's about keeping people safe, and keeping this great city and this hill as smooth running as possible."

Putnam nodded. He was beginning to see that now.

******

At 4 bells Putnam watched as the gorgeous young princess made her way to his wagon. It was far too long before he noticed that all she carried with her was her map.

As she walked up Putnam fought the urge to bow. "Did you not find your door, Miss Cynthia?"

"No." said Cynthia, "I did find every symbol but I'm afraid it was a bit of a wild goose chase." She climbed into the wagon and sat on the driver's bench.

Putnam patted the pony and climbed up beside her, his skin tingling as he brushed her elbow.

"Well," he said, as they got underway, "Do you have more to go on?"

"Actually, I do. I shall try again in the morning."

"Is there anything I could do to help?" He was hoping there was.

"Tell me, is everyone really safe in the city? I mean, if I pulled a knife right now could I really not stab you?"

"I'm afraid you couldn't. One spell or another would kick in and stop you. In the case of such a direct attack you would probably just freeze."

"You would think this was a paradise that people would flock to."

"Peace loving people do. Aggressive bullies tend to get bored and eventually tire of getting frozen and leave. I think that's why the city is full of honest hard working people. Oddly enough, I get many guests who have never heard of the spells, or the hill, or think the hill is small with just a few doors."

"I'll admit, it was ten times larger than the largest I imagined. And I saw centaurs and elves and I'm pretty sure a fairy buzzed past me."

"I wouldn't doubt it." He looked around as the pony instinctively pulled in behind another wagon. It was the end of the day and many people were heading home. After a long silence Putnam cleared his throat.

"I hope you don't mind. I spoke with a Guild member to see what was in the spot of the Beacon Star before it was built. He should be coming by tonight."

"Oh, don't mind at all, in fact I'd love hear."

"Good." Putnam smiled to himself. He had pleased the princess. It was a good feeling even if for something so small.

No one said a word the rest of the way back.

That night Horace made a hearty beef stew, this time with real beef. Putnam was half expecting his dining room to be full but the secret had yet to get out.

Cynthia came down later than expected but as it happened Tinker chose that moment to show up.

"Ah, Mr. Tinker. This is Cynthia, Cynthia, this is Mr. Tinker."

Tinker bowed and was a perfect gentleman. "My pleasure."

Putnam waved towards the empty chairs at Cynthia's table. "May we?"

Cynthia nodded and both men sat down, each was equally on their best behavior in front of such a beautiful woman.

After a long silence of just glancing at each other Tinker cleared his throat. "Well, I looked into that matter we discussed. It seems your little plot of land once played an important role in the community."

Putnam perked up. "Oh?"

"Yes, there actually was a beacon here at one time. It would have been the tallest tower in the entire village and they actually kept a fire going during the night. I couldn't really find a written description of what it looked like but the fire was mostly ceremonial, lit for important guests and occassions. It was the official beacon of Crescent. It is said that it collapsed when a Roc tried to land on it. After that, the site was cleared, it was a stable for a while, and then a cottage, which grew into the inn."

"So, there was an actual beacon here at one time?"

"It would so appear. But..."

Putnam and Cynthia leaned in, waiting for Tinker to finish.

Tinker cleared his throat again. "This was the written account. The tale of the Roc was only ninety years ago or so. We have elders twice that age."

"And?"

"Well, none of them remember a beacon. They suggest the written accounts are just off or recorded wrong, by, say, five hundred years. But as far as I can tell they are authentic, one was written by a magistrate who only passed away a few years ago. There is a discrepancy between our elders and the written record. It does not make sense."

Cynthia pulled the map from the bag at her side. She spread it out on the table. "For what it's worth this map cannot be more than 150 years old. My mother thought it was just 120 years old. In any case, there was a beacon when this map was written."

"If I may, Miss Cynthia," said Tinker, "What is your map supposed to lead to?"

Cynthia rolled her eyes to the ceiling then to the floor while sighing heavily. She wrinkled her eyebrows and finally leaned forward. "Another map. A more detailed map, one that would be hard to follow."

"And...that map?"

Cynthia rolled her eyes at the ceiling again but she realized that she had come this far, she may as well go all the way.

"Can I trust you both?"

"Madam, I am a member of the Guild. I will personally vouch for Mr. Putnam who has great integrity and as an innkeeper of the city has been trusted with many a secret before."

Putnam was a bit taken aback. He never expected such high praise from Tinker. But he nodded and returned the favor. "And Mr. Tinker is a member of the Guild, who are sworn to protect the city and its inhabitants, among other things."

Cynthia smiled a broad smile. "It is very telling that you vouched for each other and not for yourselves. There is much honor sitting at this table."

All Tinker and Putnam could think to do was nod slightly and turn bright red.

Cynthia leaned forward again. "When I was little girl I heard my father and uncle talking of the map. Just casually, mind you, as if it were just a story and they didn't seriously believe in it. Of course I was young and not paying much attention but they talked of the mountain beside our town becoming another Sugar Hill. As a child all I could think of was a mountain of sweets, it was any child's fantasy. It wasn't until I was older that I learned of your hill and it's magical properties and eventually I made the connection. When my father was old and dying I asked him if it were true and he said only if the first map were ever found. After his death I spent many years looking for the map, hidden by my great-grandfather, and found it in a very secret place in a very secret place. I had to find secret messages and solve cyphers and riddles, each pointing to the next step. All the way to the source of magic that guards the hill. A source that could be tapped, to make another Sugar Hill."

She sat back and looked out at the orange glow of sunset that was bathing the quiet street.

The two men sat in silence. Another protected hill? Was that even possible?

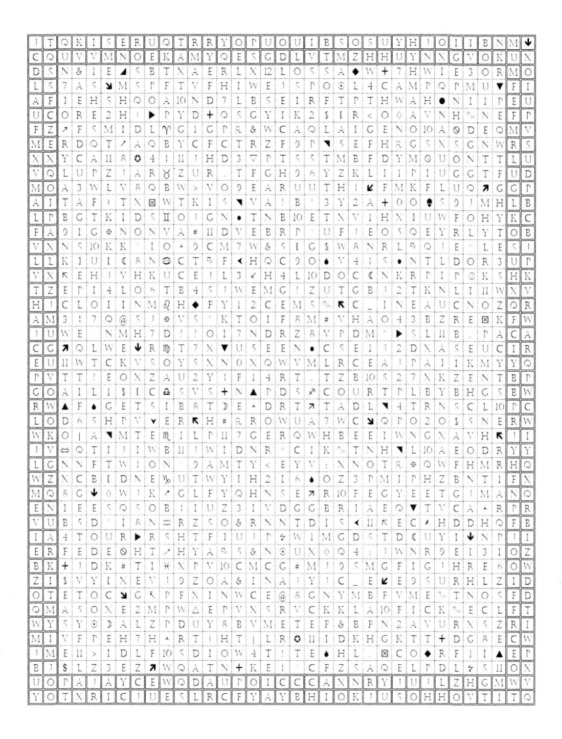

399

338

284

237

346

61

1

Cityscapes and mountianscapes,
rivers, and the trails.
Winding paths and hillsides,
a compass with no tales.
In sun or shade you can sit and
watch people going by.
The river's edge and the city's edge
spread open to the sky.
All of this and more sits
at the serpant's end.
The bigger of the two is where
I want this one to end.

001101

76

196

"You may not even realize it," Cynthia said quietly, "But you live in a paradise. If I find the second map I can make my home a paradise. No wars, no fighting. I wasn't sure I ever believed it until I actually came here and saw it myself. Back home, when I asked about Sugar Hill, and Crescent, most people just think it's all made up and that you are just a city of bankers who will do anything to please any country or race. A neutral place where kings store their gold." She waved her hand as if none of it were true. "But now I know…"

Without another word she carefully folded up her map and took her leave for the night.

For a long time Putnam and Tinker sat in silence, not even sipping their beer. Horace was nowhere to be seen and the dining room seemed strangely empty and quiet.

After a while Tinker broke the silence. "I didn't tell them." he said quietly.

"Didn't tell who what?"

"I didn't tell the Guild that we think Cynthia is Princess Gergely. As it happened I went to the archive first. When I saw the dates I thought I could ask the elders what they remembered and they denied knowing about the beacon. They acted…out of the ordinary. I played it off, saying only you wanted to know about the symbol that was on your door, that you were thinking of retiring. It was all I could think of at the moment."

Putnam wasn't sure if he should be worried or not.

Tinker went on. "I will go back tomorrow and get the names of the authors, I didn't think I'd need them. I'll see if I can track down any families or relatives that may confirm when they were written. Something very strange is going on. Very strange indeed. And while I trust the Guild with my life I can't help the feeling that they are hiding a really big secret, at least the elders are."

As Tinker got up to leave he turned to Putnam who was staring at the dirty dishes still on the table. "It may be wise to sleep with one eye open, Mr. Putnam. At least until your beautiful guest heads back to her kingdom."

Putnam half smiled. "I always take good care of my guests, Mr. Tinker. One eye and one ear…"

*****

It was nearly 4 bells before Putnam could spot Cynthia again. Unfortunately she wasn't headed his way and seemed to be making her way towards the top of the hill. If that was her, but he was certain it was as very few people were wearing purple that day. He actually felt bored, watching a princess wasn't all excitement. Still, it was shady on the side of the hill and he had some apples for company.

Off in the distance he could see Tinker shaking hands with some folks and waving at others seeming very much like his old self.

"You seem cheery," said Putnam when Tinker was in earshot.

"I am anything but, I've been up all night, I've been all over the city, and frankly, I'm exhausted." He looked around and then said, "Where is Miss Cynthia?"

Putnam looked up to where he last saw her. "She must have passed out of sight again. But don't worry, Horace is up by the water tower and he has a ruby eye, he's keeping an eye on her."

"I thought only stalkers used ruby eyes. How much does he know?"

"Everything, I trust him more than the Guild, present company excepted."

Tinker frowned. "I just may have to agree with you." He composed his thoughts and wasn't sure where to begin. "I went back to the hall of records and everything I had looked up yesterday was gone."

Putnam stopped mid bite. "What do you mean?"

"I mean it was all gone. Pages were missing from journals and what's more, the page was missing from the property book, and that book has numbered pages but the page numbers had changed. That could only be done with magic and no one is allowed magic in the hall for that very reason, we can't have records changed every time someone feels like changing the past or making a profit." He paused for a moment to let that sink in. "Don't you see? I asked about the beacon, and now all written records of it are gone."

"But why? What was so important about that beacon?"

"That's what I wanted to know. But I had to turn in reports for the day or my superiors might start to think I'm working on something that is taking all my time. So I made a golem."

Putnam was taken aback. "You made a what? That's like raising a zombie."

"No, it's fine, I dressed him up like a opener and walked him to a door that I found as a kid. A door that wasn't locked. I found it when I was little and never told anyone about it." An unlocked door wasn't unheard of but it sure was a rarity, Putnam had never come across one himself.

Tinker was trying to keep calm while explaining. "So I wrote a ticket for a simple door find, after walking around with the golem for a bit and used my own coin to pay the commission so the Guild would think I'm having a normal day. On the ticket I put contents were to be delivered to a clock shop in town."

"What do clocks have to do with anything?"

Tinker smiled. "That's the best bit. There are a number of people in this town over a hundred years old. The clock shop is a few blocks from you and have been owned by elves for almost two hundred years." He smiled even bigger. "And elves hate the Guild."

"But you're the Guild."

"Yes, but I didn't tell them that. I asked if they could tell me about the beacon, and they told me the Guild had it torn down, said it wasn't safe. The land sat empty for years, then your predecessor bought the land and built an inn. And here we are."

"But that doesn't explain anything."

"Oh, but it does. Everyone loved the beacon, it was where they had parties and ceremonies and weddings. In its last days there were near accidents, stones falling off, cracks appearing. And it was the tallest thing in the city, no one knew much about it and it was the Guild who had it torn down, it shouldn't have been any of their business, it should have been the mayor and council who decided. It was the Guild who decided that if it should fall many people could be killed, they paid for its demolition and the land. They waited a few years for people to get used to it being gone, then sold the land."

"Even back then they wanted everyone to forget it was there. And with all the people coming and going there would be no way a forget spell would work."

The two men stared at each other for a few moments, but in Putnam's mind things still weren't connecting. "What does all this have to do with the princess? And the making of a second hill?"

Tinker clapped his hands together. "I have no idea whatsoever. The Guild, as far as I know, has no idea she's here. All they know is I asked about the Beacon Star, then made sure the last vestiges of its history were erased. And look, here comes your peeping tom."

Zig zagging down the hill, Horace slowly made his way towards the two men. Slung over his shoulders were two water bags and their sloshing around was clearly annoying him to no end. Putnam had finished his apple and started another when Horace finally reached them, panting and sweating.

"I swear, coming down is harder than going up, especially with these two beasts." He plopped the bags down hard, but not so hard that they'd break open.

Putnam was looking around the hill. "Where is she?"

Still panting, Horace pointed towards the top. "At the water tower. I couldn't just hang around, I pretended I was getting some water, asked if she needed anything, then started down. You didn't want her to know we were spying on her."

"Of course not."

"She said she'd be down shortly. There she is now." Over the top of the hill a tiny purple spot appeared.

"Oh, I'd better get to the wagon." Putnam walked quickly off.

"And I need to check in." Tinker walked briskly in the other direction.

Horace, still panting, pointed towards the water bags. "But couldn't you... I mean some help..." He shook his head and grunting, threw the bags back over his shoulder.

That night there were 4 more guests in the inn and Putnam was busy with dinner and other errands but always kept one eye on Cynthia. She came back empty handed again but seemed in good spirits at first. Now she was barely picking at her dinner and she stared out the window at the inn across the street where it was loud, boisterous, and at times spilling out into the street. She waved Putnam over.

"What is all that across the street? Is it always like that?"

Putnam nodded. "That's the Singing Robin and they always draw a large local crowd."

"How come?"

"Well, they have something we don't have..."

Horace came by smiling. "Yes, big kegs of beer and huge barrels of wine."

Putnam nodded. "They also have a whole family working over there. All that has to be cleaned up every morning and they have a distillery, and it's just a bigger operation."

"You know, I feel like a little merry making tonight. You don't mind, do you Mr. Putnam?"

He shook his head. "Oh, no, I quite recommend it. Their beer is very good, we serve it here when I get the chance."

Cynthia smiled and scooted out the door. Putnam leaned over to Horace but before he could speak Horace whispered, "I should go over and keep an eye on her. I may have to drink and dance so she doesn't think anything, but it's a job I'll have to do." He set down his tray and tried to look nonchalant as he walked out the door.

Putnam wondered if he'd pass out before she came back. Shaking his head he went back to work picking up the dishes and tending to his guests.

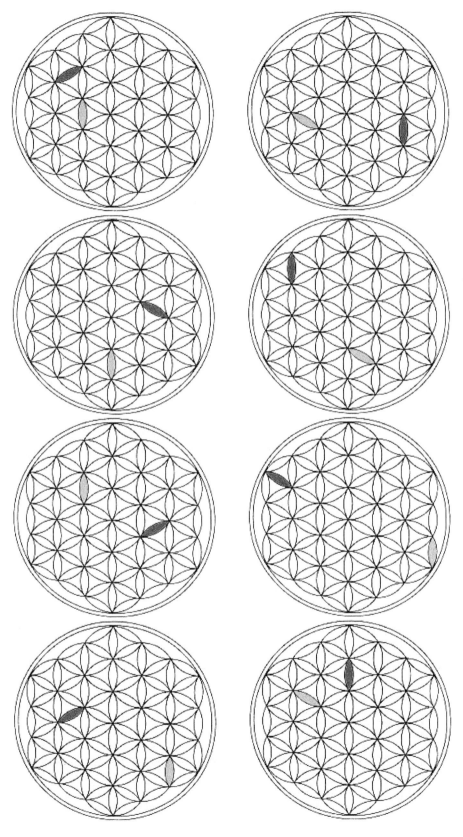

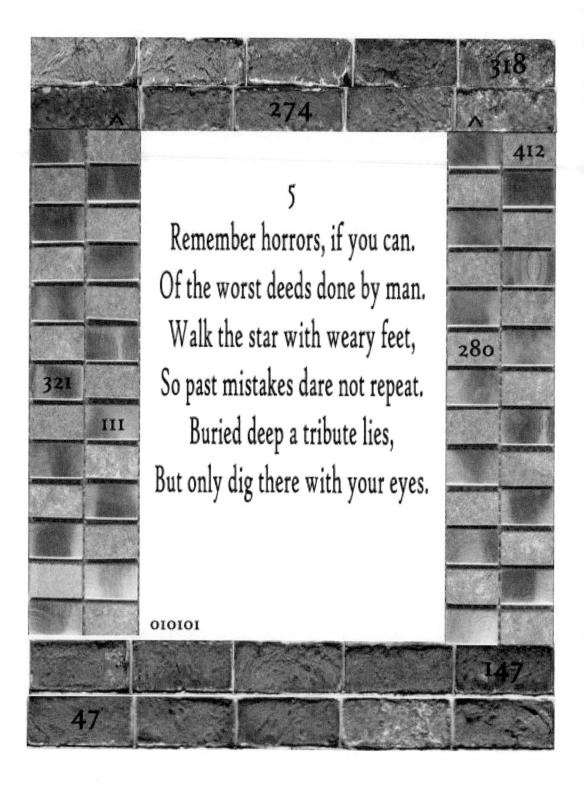

318

274

412

5

Remember horrors, if you can.

Of the worst deeds done by man.

Walk the star with weary feet,

So past mistakes dare not repeat.

Buried deep a tribute lies,

But only dig there with your eyes.

280

321

III

OIOIOI

147

47

The next morning Horace groaned and held his head as he helped four guests into the wagon. Putnam was loading lunch on the back but Cynthia was nowhere in sight and he was getting a little anxious.

Horace spotted him staring at her window. "Oh, she won't be coming. She said so last night. Said she was going to sleep all day."

This worried Putnam. "Maybe I should stay…"

"Oh…" Horace said, one hand covering his eyes. "You're not going to make me drive to the hill alone, are ya?"

"Well, I suppose not. I should, though, just on principle. Maybe I'll take the old cobblestone path this morning."

Horace moaned and fell into the back of the wagon and pulled a wool bag over his face.

The wagon pulled in later than usual, the four guests still laughing and celebrating what they had pulled from their door. Horace was dirty and sweaty and half asleep next to Putnam.

"We'd sure like to thank you, Mr. Putnam. You went above and beyond."

Putnam was tired and sweaty as well. "All in a day's work. And we always go the extra mile for our guests."

"And that you did!" The four little men leaped out of the wagon and headed across the street, there was much beer to drink and they were buying. "Come on over and have a few on us!"

Horace groaned. "Any other time I'd be right there with you, but my head still feels like a kettle of fish." He waved as they ran out of the courtyard, and was sure they hadn't heard him.

Putnam slipped out of the wagon and then leaned on it's side. "That was a lot of gold for one door. You picked a good day to be hung over, I can't remember the last time we hauled so much down the hill. And you'd think the folks at the armoury would have helped us unload it." He took a few deep breaths. "You take care of the ponies, I'll check on the guests and get supper started."

For a few long moments neither man moved. Horace looked down at Putnam, "Did you say something?"

"Ponies."

"Oh. Aye."

Putnam was surprised to find Cynthia sitting on her own in the dining room looking at a few papers she had spread around the table.

"Hello, Miss Cynthia, can I get you anything in particular for dinner? I don't think our other guests will be joining us." Indeed, his other guests were in the street already, celebrating all the gold they had.

Cynthia didn't even look up, but Putnam could still tell her face was nearly expressionless with just a hint of sadness. Still without looking up she said, "Did you ever face a task so daunting that you have to consider giving up?"

Putnam shrugged. "Not lately."

Slowly Cynthia twisted one of the papers and slid it towards Putnam. It was a grid of letters and symbols, hundreds of them, perfectly laid out. "This," she said quietly, "is a bigger map."

On the table was the first map Cynthia had, with maybe fifteen symbols total, laid out seemingly at random until you followed them. This was different, it was colder, denser. Where the other one may have been child's play this was serious business.

"I can't tell if it's a code, a walking map, some language I don't know…" She trailed off, shaking her head. "I don't recognize half these symbols." She pulled out an identical copy. "I stopped at the scribe and had him copy it. I told him it was a family code and laid out rules for the castle. I hope he bought it as I don't really want another copy floating around." She handed the copy over to Putnam. "Just in case it's ever important I wanted you to have a copy."

"I don't know what to say, are you sure it's okay?"

"The tower that was here before seemed to be important somehow. Just keep it safe, we may crack the code someday."

"I shall keep in my door, no place is safer. Like literally, the safest place in all the realms."

Cynthia smiled. She stared in sadness at the block of symbols before her then sat up and started putting her papers into her satchel. "I have to go, the reception will be starting soon."

Putnam's ears perked up. "Reception?"

"My mistress was married today. I could have never afforded a trip of this magnitude so when my mistress decided to elope I begged her take me with her. I've been her handmaiden and best friend my entire life."

"Mistress?"

"Princess Gergely. She snuck into the city a few days ago, which I hear wasn't easy."

Putnam scrunched his eyebrows together. "I thought you were Princess Gergely."

Cynthia let out a beautiful, singing laugh. "What on earth made you think that? I am Cynthia, her handmaiden. She is staying across the street, we've been sending signals through our windows, that's why I wanted a room out front."

Putnam wasn't sure he should mention the doorbell spell. "Well, there were rumors of a princess coming, And, no offense, you are beautiful and refined, and I just assumed you were incognito while looking for the map."

"Oh, my goodness, you thought I was the princess. There's just no way…" She laughed some more.

"I…I…"

"Awww…" Cynthia smiled broadly. "You thought I was the princess and kept my secret, I think that's the nicest thing anyone has ever done for me. I was right to trust you."

She gave Putnam a hug that he would remember the rest of his life, then took her leave, but not before inviting him to the reception.

While he stared at the code still sitting on the table he heard Horace moan in the kitchen. Putnam wondered if Horace could stand another night of drinking and celebrating but somehow knew he would try his best.

Putnam must have been lost in thought because the next thing he knew Cynthia was back in the dining room dressed in gorgeous silks. "Aren't you coming over?" she asked.

"Oh, yes, yes. I'll get cleaned up and be over a bit later. Just need to check the books and a few things." He rolled up the code and tapped it on the table.

She smiled and left, followed a moment later by a surprised Tinker coming in. He stopped in the doorway and watched her make her way across the street.

"She really is a lovely woman."

"Aye, that she is, that she is."

"I've no news, I'm afraid. But I still have this ominous feeling. That princess is on to something…"

"She's not the princess." Putnam interrupted.

Tinker pulled up a chair. "Come again?"

"The princess is currently across the street celebrating her elopement."

"Elopement? So that was the big conspiracy? She was trying to hide her elopement?"

"It would so appear."

"But what about the map? And the beacon? And the source of magic?" Tinker was bordering on frantic. Putnam motioned to calm down.

"The map led to a bigger map, that was complete gibberish. She is giving up on it and heading back to her family. It will probably sit in a box for another hundred years until her grand-daughter decides to figure out what it is."

"Someone at the Guild knows what it is, I'm sure. Imagine, a map showing you where the source of magic that holds the hill, nay, the whole town together. That alone would be worth all the treasures on the hill. I'd give anything to get a copy of that map, is she still here?"

Putnam glanced at the rolled up parchment in his hand. "I think it's better to lay forgotten, perhaps forever. I've seen it, it was gibberish, she wasn't sure it was a map or what. She wasn't even going to try."

"But still…"

He was interrupted again by Horace wandering in having showered and shaved and looking much better than he had before. "Evening gents. Big party across the way, I hear we are all invited."

Putnam smiled. "I don't know how you found out, but I'll be over in a bit." He looked at Tinker. "The more the merrier."

Tinker shook his head. "Oh, I don't know, I'm not much for parties, the Guild frowns on it. They don't like their members carrying on. But then again, there is a princess and it's not everyday you get to meet a princess."

Horace plopped down on a chair. "You two go freshen up and we'll head over. Be as dignified as you like, I plan on having a good time. We have no guests, the chores are done, and I can sleep till noon."

Tinker and Putnam stood up, and bowed slightly towards each other. "A night off it is."

******

The room spun and tilted wildly while the walls changed sizes and the table turned upside down.

A few more minutes should cure that, thought Horace.

Bright light was streaming in from somewhere, brighter than he had ever seen. A thousand voices were around but they started to fade.

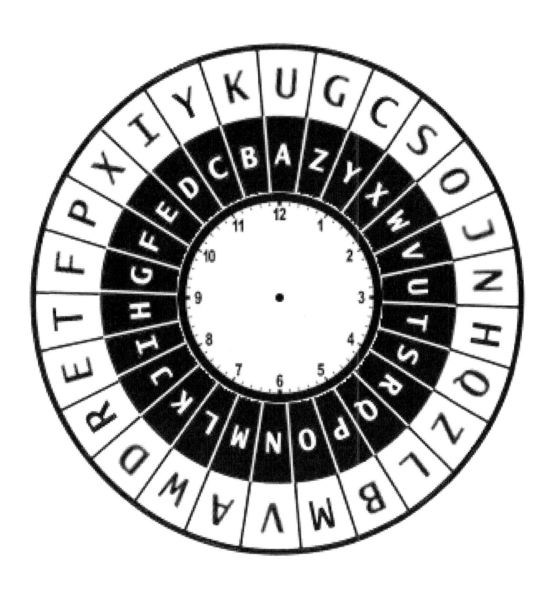

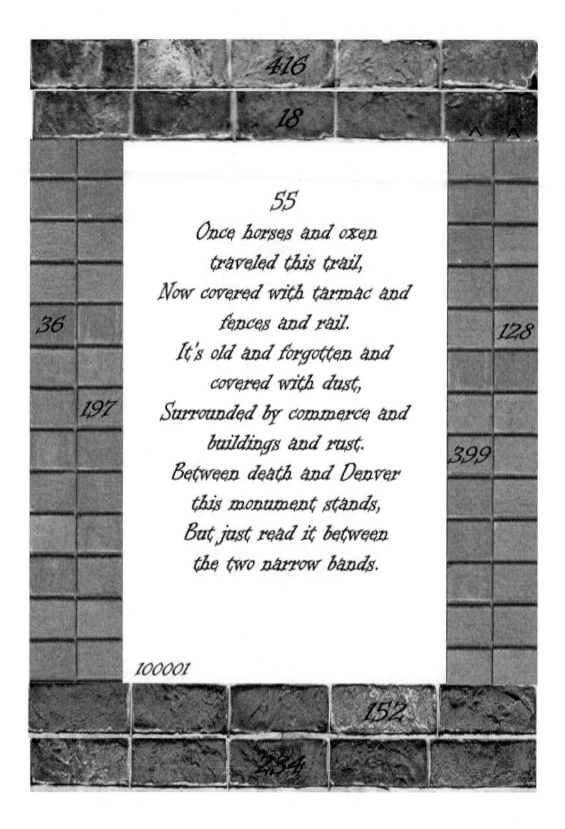

416

18

55

Once horses and oxen
traveled this trail,
Now covered with tarmac and
fences and rail.
It's old and forgotten and
covered with dust,
Surrounded by commerce and
buildings and rust.
Between death and Denver
this monument stands,
But just read it between
the two narrow bands.

36

128

197

399

100001

152

234

Somewhere deep inside him, Horace's stomach struggled with its contents. It didn't want to give up and the unpleasant thought helped Horace fight harder.

He opened one eye to try and figure out where he was. The walls tilted some more. There was a table and some chairs that didn't even slide around when the floor spun. Across the room he could make out a counter with some familiar boxes on it.

He was in the lobby of the Beacon Star.

Very carefully he lifted his head up and rested his chin on the table, which wasn't easy as his head felt as if it would explode if moved too fast. With his one open eye he took stock of the room, then did it again as he had forgotten what he was doing.

Yes, he was alone in the lobby, and this hang over would be epic. He tried to remember coming in but all he could see in his mind's eye was barrels and beautiful women. His stomach reminded him of his losing battle.

He had to do something, but what? The counter. There was something important about the counter. Behind it, in a box full of odds and ends.

The Hangover Stone.

It would calm his stomach and prevent his head from exploding. Right now it was the most powerful magic he could think of and wanted it more than anything in life even though they were common and most bars and inns had a few laying around. This one was a little more potent than the rest having come directly from Crystal Mountain and was unused when purchased.

If only he could reach it. He was sure that if he moved he would die, or at least his stomach and head would try to make him wish he would die. Was a good time like last night really worth it? He swore that if he made it to the stone he would never drink again.

Just like he had sworn fourteen times before.

He may have passed out a few more times but eventually he got his legs under him and slowly stood up and walked the ten miles to the counter. He rested his head a bit more then slid around to the back and knelt on the floor. He pulled out the first box but it was just the gold box, and it fell with a thud on the floor that rang in his head like a gong.

The next box he pulled out more carefully as it didn't have a lid and was full of odd stones and crystals. The Hangover Stone was black, and he soon found it. Well, all three.

Three? Which one was the really good one? It didn't matter, they all fit in one hand and he pulled them out and started rubbing them on his belly.

It wasn't long before his stomach and its contents settled their differences and started to relax and live in peace. It was heaven to Horace.

He let one stone drop into his other hand and started rubbing that one on his head. Whatever pressures had built up started to subside and his head felt halfway normal again.

In a few moments he was able to stand and lean on the counter, then sit in the chair behind the counter breathing a sigh of relief. He kept rubbing his head as the more he did, the more he remembered from the night before.

Crazy dances, laughter, even a kiss on the cheek. Horace smiled and relaxed some more.

After a few moments he picked up the money box and tidied up under the counter where he noticed a scroll he had never seen before.

He unrolled it on the counter and saw it was grid of symbols, most of which he had never seen before. It looked horribly complicated but just a tiny bit familiar. He dropped two of the stones back into the box but kept rubbing his head with the third, it felt so good.

He looked at the symbols, so many he had never seen before. Some he recognized from the various languages he had come across during his time at the inn, some were common symbols seen around town, like the symbol for a dead-end alley.

His eyes kept coming back to a few symbols that looked very familiar, but he couldn't place them. Somewhere he had seen these before but not in a book or on a sign. He put the stone down to smooth out the parchment but as soon as he did he lost track of what he was looking at, it became more gibberish. He picked the stone back up and started rubbing it on his head again and his train of thought came back.

He started to count various symbols, group them in his head. Somehow he knew that the Hangover Stone was allowing him to do this. As he slowly rubbed it on his head it seemed to charge his brain. He wondered if it was some sort of side effect of curing the effects of a hangover.

But that didn't seem important. What was important was that he kept coming back to a group of symbols that he knew he had seen somewhere before. Somewhere dark. Somewhere smelly. Somewhere ancient. A vision of rotten potatoes flashed through his mind. Old potatoes with long sprouts, and making out with a woman, and hiding from an argument...

The root cellar, these symbols were on the wall of the root cellar.

Grabbing a candle he went into the kitchen and threw open the cellar door.

The root cellar wasn't used much anymore and all traces of food were mostly gone and it just had some tables and chairs stacked haphazardly and a few crates of old dishes and odds and ends. He looked around at the old stone walls and for a moment couldn't remember why he came down. Then he felt the stone in his hand and began rubbing his head again. As soon as he did he realized that the old stone walls were not the same as the walls that made up the rest of building. They were far older.

It was the foundation of the old tower. He ducked under some low beams and made his way to the spot where he thought the old symbols were. Wiping away half a century of cobwebs and dust he easily found them, most likely with help from the stone reviving his memories.

One symbol was perfectly carved but the others were scratched on the stone next to it. As he stared he could picture the other symbols being expertly carved as well, but lost when the tower was torn down. Somebody had scratched them here so they wouldn't be forgotten.

Horace set the candle on a crate and pulled the scroll from his armpit and rolled it out. As he continued to rub the hangover stone on his head he searched for the symbols on the grid and found them all. With his mind's eye he connected them all and it formed a larger symbol, one he was familiar with, one that most of the town was familiar with.

It was the symbol on the main gate to Sugar Hill.

Horace felt a sense of urgency. He grabbed a satchel, put the scroll and a pencil and some bread inside, and forgetting about his chores or even where Mr. Putnam was he took a pony and rode for the main gate, rubbing his head the entire time.

The main gate was gorgeous and ornate and had guard rooms and oak doors and windows. The roof was hinged and could be opened like a drawbridge so that even the tallest folk could pass through without ducking. Guards in tall furry hats stood on either side and there were benches and lawns and every day had a festival atmosphere here.

It was mostly for the tourists.

But it could get serious, too, for this is where kings and queens would pass through with royal entourages and rich folk on faithful steeds. At the moment a large bird was being walked through led by man who looked very much like a farmer. There was no telling what you would see on any given day.

On the main part of the building, on the left side, was the symbol Horace knew was there. It had been there since the gate was built and had been painted different colors over the years, even recarved from time to time, but always stayed the same symbol. No one really knew what it meant and official word was that it was the symbol for sugar, in an ancient, forgotten language.

Still sitting on the pony, Horace unrolled the scroll, he somehow knew it would tell him what to do next. He realized this wasn't a map of the hill as he suspected, but of the town itself. It told him to go right.

He looked at the street that led off to the right. It generally marked the border of the richest, most expensive part of Crescent where kings and lords stayed and the oldest part of Crescent where ancient houses and streets stood like monuments to what the city once was. Everything here was old and sometimes crumbling, but this area was loved and was where respected people lived including many Guild members.

For a half hour he followed the clues on the map and ended up in an area where several streets met in an open area with a small fountain in the center. There were dozens of these in Crescent, and were generally places full of shops and inns. On this fine day the fountain buzzed with people from many races all carrying bags and packages and going about their business.

The map ended here and Horace wasn't sure why. The fountain was a normal stepped fountain fed from a spring and tradition was that the top steps were for drinking and the lower steps were for washing hands and ponys. This particular fountain was tall and slender and had steps that only the tallest races could reach. He thought about the princess and her people in the mountains and how none of them were particularly tall.

He got off his pony and let it drink while he went to sit on a nearby bench. People were looking at him and he realized he must seem out of place in his wrinkled party clothes from the night before and rubbing a rock on his head.

It didn't matter, though. He was deep in thought, the kind that would never come to him on even his best days. Who knew a hangover stone had such powers?

Horace heard bells and realized it past noon. He watched as the pony sidestepped a bit to keep in the shadow of the fountain while playfully dipping its nose in the water. He watched some small gnomes artfully dodge the feet of all the people that towered over them as they snaked through the market. He watched two men from a race he wasn't familiar with haggling with a tinker. They had greenish scales but big smiles.

Being in the oldest part of the town he wondered if this was the oldest fountain. Some of the steps had grooves that looked like they were carved over the course of centuries by the pouring water. There were slits at the bottom where the water disappeared and from there they would push through large underground channels that carried away sewage and rainwater. It was clever system that was copied throughout Crescent.

The pony sidestepped again and Horace followed the shadow as it lay across the cobblestone.

Then something happened. It was if Horace had been carrying a heavy bag all day and was finally able to put it down. It wasn't joy, it wasn't excitement, it was

373

161

∧

38

34

A famous place that needs no clue.

Just go there like you always do.

On the ground in front of three,

Take your pen and bend a knee.

Then take a walk, enjoy the best,

Where many men were laid to rest.

437

67

184

110111

183

378

just relief. Everything clicked together and it was like a peacefulness filled his head.

And it wasn't the rock.

Horace walked over to the pony, gave it a pet, and nuzzled it with his head, then looked deep into the waters of the steps that were low enough for him to see into. Everything was right here, in plain sight of everyone, yet no one knew it was here. He took the pencil out of his sack and wrote on the back of the scroll, then tucked them both back in, along with the hangover stone. After a while he cupped his hands and drank from the cold, falling water.

Looking around at the old shops Horace wondered why he came to this part of town. He knew he had an urge to see this fountain and it had something to do with a secret. But he was feeling deeply peaceful and simply got on the pony and rode home, noticing every beautiful thing along the way.

"Morning, Mr. Putnam!"

Putnam looked up from the table and slowly blinked. Sitting across from him was Mr. Tinker, who was staring into a cup of dark tea.

"Well, you are mighty cheerful for a man who drank his weight in wine last night. And never made it home, I see, just like Tinker here."

Horace smiled. "I did make it home, kind of, slept right where you are sitting. I woke up early and used this to it's fullest." He put the hangover stone on the table with a knock that made Tinker moan a bit.

Moving slowly, Tinker picked it up and started rubbing it on his belly. "Oh, that's the stuff." He perked up just a little bit. "The wine was good, but I think some of the food put me off."

Horace put the scroll on the table as well, then sat behind the counter and glanced at the register. "Three people checked in this morning."

"Never mind that, what were you doing with this?"

"Oh, just thought I'd give it a shot. Just a load of gibberish, I think."

"Did you tell anyone? Show anyone?"

Horace chuckle, "No, of course not. No one knows about that little bit of parchment except the three of us. And the princess."

"She's not a princess." Tinker mumbled.

There was a few moments of silence broken by Putnam. "Horace, these guests had mules, I don't suppose you're up to..."

"Say no more, I'll take care of them. And as I missed lunch I'll get started on a big supper. Something meaty." He hopped off the stool and disappeared through the kitchen.

Tinker managed a quiet hrumph. "Imagine, Horace deciphering this load of dribble."

Putnam casually unrolled the scroll and looked again at the strange symbols. Tinker sat up and pointed. "There's writing on the back."

Flipping it over, both men bent over to read the neat handwriting.

> I, Horace of the Beacon Star, do hereby state that I have found the source of all the magic that protects Sugar Hill and engulfs the town of Crescent. I now know that because it is magic that I will not remember any of this as soon as I walk away, it's the nature of this magic to protect itself, and those around it, so this memory will fade like a dream that can never be remembered.. I will also not reveal what I have seen, for the source was never meant to be searched for, as it has already been found and is shared by all. I take great comfort in knowing that it is safe and will be around for a long, long time to come and I know that the people of Crescent, it's citizens and guests and all that visit this strange hill are the greatest in all the lands in all the worlds. The true adventure is living.

Both men sat with their jaws opened wide.

"That damned fool did it. Somehow that damned fool did it."

Tinker looked up at Putnam. "Should we tell him?"

Putnam nodded. "Hell, yes, I'm telling him." He fell silent for a few moments. "Well, maybe not today. But I will."

"You know, if he knows he found it once he may go crazy trying to find it again. He may become a man obsessed."

"Maybe." Putnam rolled the scroll up as tight as he could. "For now I'm putting this in my door. Today. It needs to be safe, and there's no where safer."

"Agreed. I don't think even the Guild should know about this. They wouldn't rest, either, if they knew. And they certainly wouldn't leave Horace alone."

"Yes." Putnam slowly stood up and grabbed the hangover stone and put it back into it's box under the counter and set the scroll down beside it.

"Let me clean up, and I'll give you a ride home."

Tinker sat up and smiled. "Well, for once I'm a paying guest, I'll stay for supper. I think I deserve a day off. Tomorrow I'll be back on the hill doing what I do best."

Putnam smiled. "Overcharging for common advice?"

"At least I know I'll have job security for a long, long time. And the Beacon Star and it's guests will get my secret ten percent discount."

"I'd drink to that, but I don't think I can look at a mug of ale for a few nights yet."

"Or wine."

"Well, let's not get too hasty…"

RANDY R PISCHEL

If you liked this book then you can also check out:

Three Men in a Tub by Randy R Pischel,
exclusively on Amazon
Rebecca's Lament by Rebecca Best,
exclusively on Kindle
A Year in Afkear by Edith Telegrafi
Exclusively on Amazon

For More Mysteries Look For:

The Last Key of Solomon on YouTube
CryptoTweets on Twitter,
the official Twitter for this book.

Printed in Great Britain
by Amazon